THE Charming THIEF

TAYA RUNE

Taya Rune

The Charming Thief

Copyright © 2021 by Taya Rune.

For information contact :
purplerealmpublishing@gmail.com
ISBN: 978-1-922604-13-2 (ebook)
ISBN :978-1-922604-18-7 (paperback)
First Edition: November 2021

Purple Realm Publishing

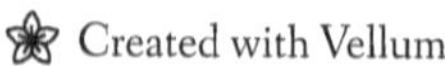 Created with Vellum

THE Charming THIEF

TAYA RUNE

Purple Realm
PUBLISHING

To all the princesses who chose their own fate.

CHALLENGE ISSUED
FLORIAN

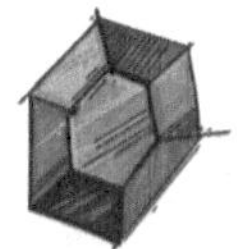

Prince Florian, the third-born son of the ruling family of the Kingdom of Dreams, pressed his tongue against the roof of his mouth in an effort to stop his mouth from stretching wide in a yawn. It was a trick his mother had taught him when he was younger and had been taken to task by his governess when she had caught him dropping his head at court one day to try to hide what was happening. Florian had complained to his mother, as how was he expected to not yawn? The ever-clever Queen had given him her secret. He clamped his jaw shut but forced his lips into a pleasant smile as the next courtier was presented to his father, mother, and the remainder of his assembled family. His middle brother, Prince Phillip, and his beautiful betrothed, the ruler of the Land of the Moors, Queen Dawn, were the guests of honor today, so sat next to the king and queen. While Florian stood to the right and slightly behind Queen Dawn, his eldest brother, Prince Henri, stood to the left and slightly behind the King's throne, as he was the next in line, and standing beside Henri was Princess Ashe, Henri's wife. The dais was crowded today.

As the fawning courtier and his heavily jowled and atrociously bejeweled wife gave their final subservient bow, their plain-faced daughter stared unashamedly at Florian as they backed away to find their assigned place in the throne room. He was now the only single royal family member and his reputation as a lover was an enticing combination to many women in the court, which he typically played upon.

His hazel eyes swept the room, taking little notice of the bright banners and standards with the country's noble families' emblems emblazoned upon them. His eyes only skimmed over the tall, carved, and deeply polished columns that held the vaulted ceiling in place and the stained-glass windows that sat high near the roof that threw a beautiful and colorful spectrum of light across the crowded room. He was thinking of the previous evening's escapades in the private garden of the capital's richest merchant. The night had been balmy and the surroundings pleasant as he had engaged in some glorious heavy petting with the merchant's gorgeous and off-limits daughter.

Excited whispers filled the room as the gathered crowd of nobles turned back expectantly toward the Master of Ceremonies. The next visiting noble to be presented on this auspicious occasion was announced, and the whispers grew into louder babble as each person exchanged what they knew about the latest arrival with their neighbor.

They all strained their necks in the hope to be the first to catch a glimpse of the much gossiped about Queen of the Fourth Kingdom as the large double doors slowly swung inward to reveal seven large, and Florian noted extremely handsome men standing in a tight formation. At the click of the front guard's heels, the other six men took a step outward and revealed a small, dark-haired woman in an unusual dress. Florian kept his features smooth as he took in the colorful gown; it was different from what any of the other nobles here in the Kingdom of Dreams wore, and he wondered if this is what was normal attire for the nobility in the Fourth Kingdom. The dress had a sunshine-yellow full skirt, a bright blue fitted top with puffed sleeves, a high white collar, and a rich, red cape. The Queen of the Fourth Kingdom was almost a walking rainbow, and the only reason it didn't look ludicrous on her was the way in which she held herself as she stepped out of the circle of her body-guards and glided down the long aisle to the waiting king and queen.

Florian was no longer disinterested in the proceedings. This woman was mesmerizing, and he had to have her. All thought of pursuing the merchant's pretty daughter disappeared, and a need to know and possess this beauty became his goal.

Queen Wynter did not curtsy as she reached the raised platform. She instead nodded her head to each of the seated royals and to Prince Henri; her eyes only skimming over Florian, much to his chagrin. All muttering ceased within the cavernous throne room as the seated members on the dais rose with respect and bowed their heads to the queen who had thwarted the evil woman who had tried to kill her to usurp her throne. It was rumored that the true reason wasn't to take the throne, but that the stepmother had become obsessed with her own appearance as she aged and had been told Wynter would one day blossom and surpass her beauty so had cold heartedly ordered Wynter killed. The huntsman that was supposed to take her into the woods to kill her was too soft hearted and had let Wynter run away instead. Florian wondered how much of that story was true and how much was gossip that had been changed as it was spread. Though, if he did remember that story correctly she had been rescued by a passing prince who had kissed her to wake her from the curse that had been placed on her, just like his sister-in-law to be Queen Dawn.

All eyes were focused on the newly crowned queen, so Florian took the opportunity to admire her obvious charms. *Oh, this is going to be fun,* he thought to himself as he took in her perfect features and curvy figure. As the pleasant greetings came to an end Queen Wynter was escorted to a seat close to the front, but where her seven strapping body-guards could fan out behind her, Florian forced himself to focus once again on the boring procession of visiting nobles that had come for his brother's betrothal ceremony. Though his eyes did linger on her face as she settled into her seat, and he caught and held her attention for a fraction longer than was entirely proper, he did, in the end, turn back to the next noble now walking down the aisle. He could have continued to stare at her and take in her pure beauty as she sat regally to one side for several candlemarks, but he was too well-trained to give in to his longing. The games would begin later.

*T*he applause was resounding and satisfying, and Florian paused as he entered the tavern, a flower stem caught between his teeth. He took the pale pink rose from his mouth and bowed deeply with a sweeping gesture before standing and straightening his black velvet doublet with its silver trim, and offered the rose to a middle-aged woman who sat laughing with her husband near the door. She blushed at the gesture, which made him give her a wicked grin and earned him a flat stare from her balding partner. Florian winked at the man and knew that one of his two bodyguards would smooth things over by offering to buy him a tankard of mead once the prince moved on.

"I have no idea what that was for," he lied to the tavern goers. "But I thank you for the warm welcome."

This drew laughter and further catcalling from a few rowdy patrons as most had heard the boast he had made to his best friend, Stic, only a few nights prior. He had claimed that he would gain an invitation to the Master Merchant's family home and pluck a rose from the family's fabled, secluded, and much-talked-about internal rose garden. When Stic had asked how he would know if Florian had completed the issued challenge, the prince had said that he would get the pretty daughter of the merchant to personally give him a rose after he kissed her in the aforementioned garden.

Florian sat down in the chair opposite his waiting friend and adjusted the sword that hung at his side so it sat more comfortably. "It would seem you have again lost another wager," the too-handsome prince spoke as he waved his hand to summon the serving girl. "A tankard of mead for my friend and me," he ordered.

The small tavern, with its clean tables and decent food and ale, was a popular place for the younger nobles of the city. It afforded them a relatively safe place to find entertainment while getting away from the ever-watchful eye of their parents. The other patrons of the place had a clear understanding that whatever was said or occurred in the Wild Ram stayed within the walls of the Wild Ram. Early on, there had been several mishaps and unusual happenings to those who spoke out of turn, and that now kept everyone in check without anything needing to be done or said. The owner, Eli, had made it clear that there were to be no weapons in the place, nor bodyguards; but the prince was the prince, and like everything else in his small world, the rules didn't apply to him.

The serving girl returned with their drinks and Stic paid for them, as was the norm when he lost a wager.

After taking a long draught of the drink, Stic wiped his hand across his mouth and sat back in his chair. "I think I have come up with the ultimate challenge for you, if you care to really test your metal and skill."

"I find that hard to believe," scoffed Florian as he winked at the serving wench behind the bar, only half paying attention to his friend. "Besides, I have already issued myself a new conquest."

Stic laughed and took a swig of his heavy mug. "Really? And what is your reward?"

Florian looked to his friend and took in his mischievous green eyes and blonde, closely trimmed beard. "Truthfully, I think she is the conquest and the reward."

The smaller man moved closer to his friend and said in a low voice, "I was thinking that this challenge might be big enough that it may earn you the reward you have been wanting since you learned my secret." He arched an eyebrow at him. "You have been trying to gain it for so long."

"Maybe I don't want it anymore." Florian tried to look nonchalant, but they both knew it to be false. That, after all, was Stic's gift. Somehow, he always knew the truth.

Stic sat back in his chair as the serving girl placed Florian's customary plate of cold meat, cheese, and warm bread on the table. "So, you are not even mildly interested in my challenge? It has a time factor, a seduction, and a heist, and if you do it all without being caught and imprisoned, or hung, I promise to give you what you want."

Florian's curiosity was peaked. He wanted to know what the challenge was, and his ego was not going to let him walk away once he did. Instead of taking the bait, he slowly carved a piece of cheese and piled it onto a chunk of bread then added a thick slice of cured meat. The prince chewed slowly, knowing that it would irritate his friend. They both knew, in the end, he would hear the challenge and as he had never backed down from one, he would accept it, but this time it was for much higher stakes. If Stic felt he could bet the ultimate prize as a reward, he must be fairly confident that Florian would not be able to complete the challenge. "So, we know what you will give me if I win, but what do you want from me in the highly unlikely event I lose?" Florian asked as he took up his cup.

The attractive, smaller man with his sharp features and perfect smile leaned in and whispered in Florian's ear.

"What I have always wanted." His breath was hot, and Florian tried to ignore the unexpected flush of desire that crept through his body. "You." Stic sat back in his chair and slowly traced his index finger around the top of his goblet as he watched the prince through his blond eyelashes.

This statement should have shocked Florian, but somehow he had always known that this was Stic's end game, just as much as what he wanted from his friend was his own. "So this is it? The time has come?" He cut another slice of cheese as if nothing out of the ordinary had been spoken.

Stic broke eye contact and indicated to the girl behind the bar that they each needed another drink. "Are you interested in those terms?"

"As I have never failed a challenge you have set, I think I can be confident in being amenable to your conditions, but let us hear the impossible task first."

"That is only fair. You have five days, as that is how long the celebrations will last, to seduce three women of my choosing. You must also discover their most valuable possession, steal it, and give it to me. My powers are minor, but I can determine if it is indeed their most coveted item."

Florian considered it. Seducing three women into giving him their secret was not as difficult as most would think. While his older brothers had concentrated on being good soldiers and princes, he had decided to use his good looks and charming ways for his own gratification, and had learned how to get a woman to do what he wanted with very little effort. "That's it? There must be a bigger catch?"

Stic shrugged, but didn't elaborate or give anything away. Florian thought the wager over and then he paused as

Stic's words sunk in. He would choose the women. "Who are the three women? I have standards to maintain, you know."

"They are all beautiful, noble, and within your acceptable age bracket. It wouldn't be much of a challenge if I wanted you to sleep with someone desperate—that would make it too easy for you." Stic was clearly enjoying himself as he drained the tankard and started on the fresh one that had been placed before them. "You up for the challenge?"

"Who are the women?"

"You have to accept to find out."

Florian stopped chewing and watched a slow grin make its way across his friend's features. There was something he wasn't telling him, but he would only know what it was once he agreed to the terms of the bet. He needed to know who these women were. Damn Stic and his clever manipulation of the prince's need to never back down and be the best at whatever he did. Without further preamble, Florian stuck out his hand. "On the condition you give me all three names now."

Stic took the proffered hand and they both solemnly shook. The agreement had been made. "You must seduce and bring me the most valued item of Queen Wynter."

The prince kept his features serene. Queen Wynter was who he had planned to bed anyway; adding the theft of a trinket would be no hardship. This was going to be easy. They kept their arms clasped together as Stic announced the second woman. "Queen Dawn."

Florian tried to keep his face from showing any surprise as Stic named the woman who had just become engaged to his brother, and who all the nobles of the Kingdom of

Dreams and surrounding nations had come to celebrate the betrothal of. How was he going to get her into his bed? He didn't doubt his ability to do it, just that it could be done in five days. A twisted thought entered his head as he considered who the final woman would be. Suddenly, the idea of the stakes took on a whole new meaning. It was not going to be as easy to earn his prize from Stic as he originally thought. "Let me guess.' Florian let a sly smile play on his full lips, not showing anything other than bravado at the situation; though, if he took a moment to reflect on how he felt, he would have to admit his heart was beating a little quicker with the anticipation of what was to come. "The third woman you want me to sleep with and steal from is my sister-in-law, Princess Ashe?"

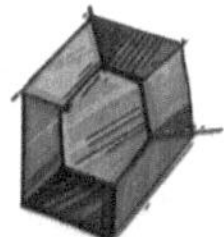

The arrow struck the bullseye and the crowd cheered. It was the first bullseye for the tournament, and Prince Phillip had been the one to accomplish it. He smiled and waved to the assembled nobles and rich merchants who were in attendance. Florian took little notice of the goings-on as he swung his arms in wide arcs before holding one arm across his chest and then the other as he stretched his muscles. Phillip had been the fourth to compete, Henri would be the sixth, and Florian would be last, in twelfth. The rest of the competing field was made up of ruling nobles or their sons looking to impress the king.

Phillip was an above-average archer, but where he excelled was with a heavy sword and shield. He had proven himself by slaying a dragon. Even though, technically, it had been a witch transformed into a dragon, it had still had razor-sharp teeth, breathed fire, and was larger than the average barn. Phillip had declared he wanted to compete in the archery tournament as he would not be hunting on the morrow and wanted to mix with those that had come to celebrate his engagement.

Henri was a better archer than Phillip, and Florian took him more seriously when he stepped up to take his turn. He stopped his stretching and moved to the front of where all the competitors had gathered, no one telling him off for standing in front of them. There were always perks to being the third born to the king. Florian applauded with the rest after Henri's five shots put him in first place.

"What do you think? Can you beat your brothers today, Prince Florian?" An older man came up and stood to one side, his shoulders slightly hunched, and he squinted up at the prince.

He avoided the question. "Viscount George, it is a pleasure to see you here. And who have you brought with you to compete?" Florian looked at the young man, on the other side of the Viscount, he was barely out of his teens, confidently holding his bow in one hand.

"Allow me to introduce my nephew, Pierre. He will inherit when I am gone. He is my sister's boy and the smartest out of the bunch; thankfully, he was born first."

Florian inclined his head, while Pierre bowed deeply. "It is an honor, Your Highness."

"You any good with that?" Florian nodded toward the bow.

The young man, who was only a few years younger than Florian, shrugged in the typical fashion of someone completely competent with their weapon but did not want to seem boastful. "I shoot well enough that I shall never go hungry."

Florian laughed. "A fine answer."

Pierre looked happy with the minor praise. "I am up next, wish me luck," the dark-featured, young gentlemen said.

"I get the feeling you are not going to need it."

Florian watched Pierre move out into the sunlight and stand on the line that they all must shoot from. Henri and Phillip came to stand beside him, and the Viscount greeted them both, explaining who Pierre was, though they hadn't asked. Pierre lined up and notched his arrow. His first shot hit the bullseye and the crowd responded loudly. His next two shots hit the middle ring, then his next shot scored him another bullseye and his final one earned him an inner ring. This moved him up into second position.

"He shoots well," Florian commented to Viscount George. "If he widened his stance a little and brought his elbow in a fraction more he could be exceptional."

Both the older princes agreed. It didn't take long until Florian's turn came around. Henri was still sitting in first, with Pierre in second. Phillip was fifth. The first round saw the field of competitors halved at the end of it. So both his brothers were already through. Florian just needed to beat the man currently in sixth to qualify.

With minimum fuss, Florian stood at the line and fired his five arrows in a steady motion. Each arrow landed precisely where he wanted it and he left the field to polite applause and having qualified to the next round in sixth place.

Drinks were circulated and money changed hands as bets were laid for the next round after seeing the competitors perform in the first round. Henri was now favorite as he sat in first. This round was like the last, after everyone had shot five arrows the field was halved. This would leave the final three for one last round, where the targets became harder to hit.

As the leader, Henri went first and performed well. He managed three bullseyes, each one drawing a louder yell of appreciation from the crowd until his fourth shot went horribly wrong and hit the outer ring. The ripple of disappointment that ran through the spectators was palpable. His final shot hit the middle ring.

Next, Pierre came to the line and again impressed the crowd with his efficient shooting. Florian noted his stance was a little wider. Obviously, Viscount George had taken Florian's observations seriously and had advised his nephew accordingly. The tightening of his elbow would take readjusting and practice for it to have any real effect, so he hadn't changed that. Pierre now sat in the lead, two points clear of Prince Henri. The third and fourth competitors failed to perform under pressure and Phillip moved to take his turn. He managed two bullseyes and several inner rings, and now sat in third.

It was finally Florian's turn. As Phillip walked back and Florian moved out into the sun they crossed paths. Phillip held out his hand to his youngest brother. Florian grasped Phillip's forearm in a firm hold and smiled at him. "Sorry, big brother."

Phillip laughed one of his rare laughs. "No, you're not."

Florian chuckled. "You're right. I'm not." They let go and went on their way. As Florian came to stand at the line, he settled his breathing and blocked out the sounds that surrounded him. He raised the bow and notched the first arrow deciding on how he would play this. He let the arrow fly and it went wide. Missing everything and landing with a twang in the trunk of a tree behind the target.

The crowd gasped and Florian dropped his head so they couldn't see his smirk. Raising his head, his face serious, a look of worry plastered across his handsome features, he took another arrow. This one he let fly and knew it would hit the inner ring. Now he needed three bullseyes and he would be sitting in equal second with his brother, Henri. With casual grace, Florian hit the bullseye all three times, just as he needed, and the gathered nobles shouted enthusiastically.

With there being no third, it was mentioned that they should perhaps draw straws to see who would go second and third; Florian declined and offered to go last.

All three men watched silently as the target was moved further back and another challenge was being set up next to it. The new challenge came in the shape of a scarecrow; it had a red spot, roughly the same size as the bullseye painted on the center of its chest and face. There were three mannequins: one for each contestant.

Henri and Florian stood patiently as they looked on as Pierre walked to the line and placed seven arrows in the quiver he wore strapped to his back. "Who do you think will win?" Henri asked him.

"Honestly?"

Henri raised his eyebrows at him. "Care to make it interesting?"

"Sure, you know I won't back down from a wager. What did you have in mind?"

"I win and you will owe me one favor to be determined at a later time. If you win, I owe you the favor."

"What happens if he wins?" Florian nodded his head toward Pierre, who was in the middle of shooting his five arrows at the target.

"You really think he will win?" Henri scoffed quietly.

"Fair point." Florian held out his hand to his eldest brother. "Deal."

"Deal." They shook hands as the nobles applauded Pierre as he completed his round.

Florian was impressed as he noted four arrows sticking out of the bullseye and one from the inner ring. The scarecrow had its heart pierced perfectly, but the arrow to the head was just slightly off target. He clapped with the rest as Pierre came to stand next to him, and Henri made his way to the line.

Pierre looked pleased with himself as he turned to watch the prince. Florian watched with an impassive face as Henri hit four bullseyes, one inner ring. He was even with Pierre so far. Henri paused a few moments with his arrow notched and aimed at the mannequin. He let the arrow soar and it landed with a thud into the center of the dot that filled the face of the stuffed dummy. Muttering and whispering grew as more wagers changed hands as Henri prepared for his final shot. He notched the arrow and Florian smiled as he watched the arrow fly smoothly toward the mannequin. It hit the center of the chest and the crowd erupted with cheers as the popular prince had moved to the front of the winner board.

"Well, we tried," Pierre announced as if Florian had already been defeated.

"Keep your elbow tucked in like I told your uncle," Florian responded as he moved to take his place at the line.

"Bravo, my brother," He congratulated Henri as he moved out the way.

Henri smiled. "I am trying to decide what favor I need from you," he gloated.

"I'll be back in a minute, so keep thinking about it," Florian said airily.

A hush fell over the gathered people and most dismissed the prince as he had not managed to beat either of his opponents in the other rounds. Florian chose seven arrows from the pile on the table and placed them in his quiver. He looked to his right and saw the beautiful face of Queen Wynter, seated on a high-backed chair at the front of the crowd and surrounded by four of her burly body-guards. He had known she had been there the whole time, but he had chosen not to acknowledge her till now. He nodded to her formally and she graciously returned the gesture.

Florian turned back to face the targets and took in a strong, steadying breath. He narrowed his gaze for a moment, solely focused on the small black dot in the middle of the target. Settling his mind, he began to count in his head. On the fourth count he withdrew the arrow, notched, and released all in a smooth motion. Florian repeated the process for all seven arrows. As the final arrow found his target he turned to face Wynter before it had even reached its mark.

The crowd roared as the seventh arrow found its perfect target, just as the other six had. This time, Florian bowed to the Queen of the Fourth Kingdom. She laughed and smiled in response.

Many people came up to congratulate him, including

his brothers. Henri slapped him on the back. "I had no idea."

Phillip laughed. "I did." Henri looked surprised, while Phillip shrugged. "Our brother is full of surprises. Never underestimate him."

Henri nodded as if only now realizing his baby brother had grown up. "I won't."

F lorian dropped his head and groaned with a combination of pleasure and pain as he leaned into the hands that massaged his right shoulder. He had twinged his shoulder while showing off at the archery competition. There had been no need for him to shoot in rapid succession, but showing Henri up had been irresistible. He sat straddled over a chair, his bareback to the entrance of the royal pavilion, ignoring the tut-tutting of Tumas, his long-suffering manservant.

Tumas was a decade older than Florian and had become his manservant when Florian had turned sixteen. He had had to add a few skills to his normal ones as Florian accepted more daring challenges and would come home scraped, bruised, and occasionally lacerated from the daredevil stunts he agreed to. Rather than send him off to the palace chirurgeon for a lecture and then having to explain his actions to his father, Tumas had become proficient in cleaning and sewing his lord back together. But the price of Tumas's silence was having to endure his tut-tutting at what he perceived as Florian's foolishness and hubris.

"That should do it," Tumas said in his deep, rumbling

voice, that as far as Florian was concerned, matched his shaggy dark features; though, he did try to look tidy by tying his long hair back in a ponytail at the nape of his neck. Tumas wiped his hands on a cloth and put the liniment oil and soiled linen back into the box they had been taken from.

Florian stood and slowly rotated his shoulder and then lifted his arm. "You are a magician, Tumas." There was no niggling or pulling feeling anymore.

Without fanfare, the tent flap was pulled open and Queen Dawn stepped through, and halted immediately. She blinked to allow her vision time to adjust to the darker space of the tent from the intense brightness of the hot sun outside. Finally, she took in the view of the two men and her eyes grew wider for a second as she looked at Florian standing there shirtless. Quickly, she averted her eyes. "I did not mean to intrude."

"Tumas here was just about to start lecturing me on my impulsive need to take everything one step too far. You have not intruded but saved me." Florian raised an eyebrow at his servant.

The large man shook his head in defeat before turning to the beautiful queen. "May I offer Your Majesty a seat and refreshment? It is an exceptionally humid day and I am sure you are not used to this heat, coming from a little further north."

Florian grabbed his tunic but caught Dawn sneaking a look at him. Instead of putting it on, he carried it loosely in his hand, so if someone walked in he could make a show of putting it on. "I can take care of our guest, Tumas."

It was clear to all three people in the tent that that was a clear dismissal. "Go have something to eat and drink; enjoy flirting with a pretty wench, if she'll let you."

"Thank you, Your Highness."

Florian took the goblet from his servant's hand and watched the bulky man walk out, pulling the tent flap down as he went. "Your Majesty looks a little hot and bothered. What would you like to drink?" He held up the empty cup.

"Please call me Dawn. Do you have any pear cider? I have grown quite fond of it."

"Certainly. It is my mother's favorite too."

As Florian found and poured the cider, Dawn moved deeper into the large royal tent. With its rich rug covering the majority of the dried grass, a long table with plenty of chairs, and even a make-shift bed set up in one corner, it was a haven from the outside world and the heat. She trailed her hand along the back of the chair he had been sitting on earlier. "You were impressive today."

He inclined his head in acknowledgment as he put the stopper of the bottle back on. He watched the queen fan herself with her hand. "Do you ever get used to this heat?"

Florian laughed. "Some do, some don't." He walked over to her and handed her the goblet.

She stopped fanning herself and took the drink. "Thank you."

Dawn was shy, sweet, and naive, and although they had spent a small amount of time together when she had been awakened by his brother, he had not had the chance to truly get to know her. At the time, he had been bitter at being left behind to guard her while Phillip had gone off to kill the witch who had turned herself into a dragon, come back the conquering hero, and then claimed his kiss from the slumbering beauty. No one knew how often Florian had dreamt about being the one to lean over the delicate sleeping woman and kiss her soft lips.

A thought crossed his mind as he took in the flushed cheeks of the Queen of the Moors. Her oval face and cornflower blue eyes matched her mid-length, blonde hair perfectly. She wore her hair down and a small gold coronet, rather than the large, gold crown she had worn while she slept and waited for the curse to be lifted. As she sipped her cider, Florian moved to the area where the bed was and opened a chest. Right on top were several fans that his mother utilized when it got hot. Florian chose a fan that would match Dawn's soft yellow gown with its yellow and rose gold threaded sunrises that adorned the hem of the full skirt.

"Here, this might help." He held the fan out to the queen.

"Are you sure?"

"Absolutely. Mother taught me to be a gentleman, and a gift from one queen to another in need is appropriate."

Dawn placed the drink on the nearby table and came to take the fan. She snapped it open and began to cool herself, her hair moving gently with the wind she created. The movement of her hair, her parted lips, and the look of bliss that crossed her beautiful face made his cock twitch. The familiar tingle of desire ignited in his gut, and he knew bet or no bet, he wanted her.

"There are times when I wish it was me who had kissed you." The words were barely above a whisper. "That I had slain the dragon and come to your rescue." He raised his hazel eyes and met her blue ones, daring her to look away.

"Maybe you could have rescued me from myself if I had just kissed you?"

Queen Dawn blinked several times, but she did not break his stare. Florian knew her breathing had deepened by the rise and fall of her breasts. She still held the fan, but it had stilled. He wanted to close the gap between them and kiss her but knew it was too soon. She would run. Instead, he stood still, willing her to say something. "Your brother is a good man."

Not what he wanted to hear, but it wasn't unexpected. He knew from seducing other betrothed women that they were, at this point, talking more to themselves than to him. Trying to remain faithful while being tempted with something deliciously forbidden was difficult. "He is a good man," he agreed. "But a tad stoic and boring."

"Phillip always tries to do the right thing," she said with very little conviction.

Florian leaned forward a fraction and did not break eye contact. "Do you ever wish it had been me?"

Dawn blinked rapidly, and he held his breath. After several moments she spoke. "Thank you for the thoughtful gift."

"I hope you think of me and what could have been when you use it."

She brushed her lips against his cheek and whispered. "I will."

"Do you?" he asked as she pulled away.

"Do I what?"

He unleashed his most disarming smile. "Play the what-if game?"

"I must go and get ready for this evening's state dinner."

Her eyes flickered to his bare chest, and he noted her free hand flex as if she forced it to remain still.

"You know by not answering and avoiding the question, in essence, you have answered me?" He stepped back, breaking the intimate connection they had formed by standing so close. "I would hope you honor me by saving me one dance at the ball?"

Dawn smiled widely and his stomach tightened. "Of course. It is expected that I should dance with my betrothed's brother; though, I am a terrible dancer."

Florian laughed. She was subtly flirting with him and he loved it. If he had weeks, he was confident that he would be able to have his way with her, but he only had four more days, so he was going to have to plan his next step carefully.

His next words were interrupted by the sound of approaching men. Florian took another step back and put his shirt on. "Someone is coming," he told her.

"You heard that?"

"Years of practice." He didn't add why he had needed the skill. "Well, I am off to bask in the rewards of winning against my brothers." He winked at her as he rose the flap and then spoke loudly. "Your Majesty." He bowed and dropped the material.

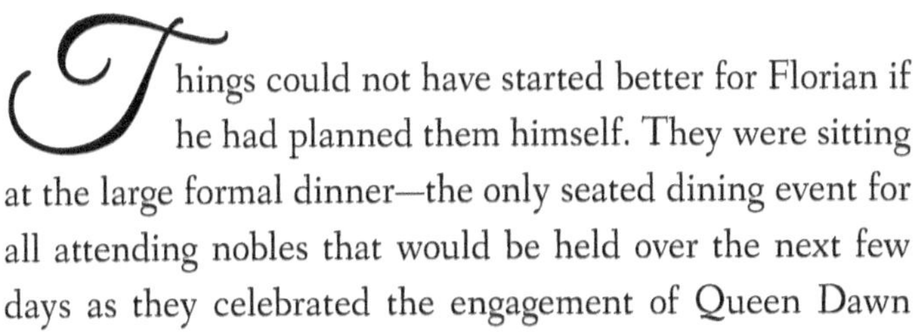

*T*hings could not have started better for Florian if he had planned them himself. They were sitting at the large formal dinner—the only seated dining event for all attending nobles that would be held over the next few days as they celebrated the engagement of Queen Dawn and Prince Phillip. The wedding of the queen and her soon-to-be prince consort would happen in Dawn's own lands where the fairy folk of the Moors could also attend. That was planned for six months from now. This occasion was not only to celebrate the engagement of the couple but to show the unity between the lands and to farewell the beloved second Prince of the Kingdom of Dreams.

Florian found himself seated between his sister-in-law, Princess Ashe, and Queen Wynter. Both women were on Stic's seduction list, and Florian had to admit sitting in between these two beauties was a blessing. This would be a perfect opportunity to get them talking about their most valued possession, if he could steer the conversation in that direction. His brother, Prince Henri, and husband to Ashe, was seated on the other side of his wife and next to their father, and Florian knew from experience that Henri and the king would engage in political discussions all evening and bore everyone with their words. Florian might even be able to get a little subtle flirting in. As Henri would be so absorbed in pleasing their father that he would be taking very little notice of his wife and youngest brother.

Queen Wynter was stunning in a shimmering snow-white gown, that gave the illusion that her pure white skin glowed too. Her shiny black hair was held back by a diamond tiara and her lips were full and candy apple red. Her words were soft and clipped in an accent he found alluring, and her large brown eyes hinted at mischief and merriment. He noted that only one of her strong, tall body-guards stood behind her chair, his arms crossed and a scowl on his chiseled features. No weapons were allowed in the presence of the royal family, but Florian had the feeling this man could stop just about anything that attempted to attack his queen.

"Would it be inappropriate of me to tell you that you look beautiful this evening, Your Majesty?" Florian raised his silver goblet in salute to Wynter.

She, in turn, picked up her goblet in response and smiled sweetly at him. "Yes, it would."

Florian feigned horror at his faux pas. "Can you forgive my innocent remark? I but only speak the truth, Your Majesty."

Queen Wynter paused in mid-drink and studied the prince over the rim of her cup. "I am not sure I should, but we certainly don't need an embarrassing incident for the royal family so soon after my arrival."

"How do you think I can make it up to you?" he asked.

If she had been anyone other than a visiting monarch, he would have placed his hand on her thigh to indicate where his thoughts were going. No one would be able to see it; even though the main table faced the rows of guests, there was a long overhanging tablecloth so his mother could remove her shoes without anyone realizing it. Instead, he smiled in his most charming way and waited for her response.

"Let me think about it."

Before he could come up with a witty rejoinder, the servants began to file in through a side door with platters of steaming food, and her attention was drawn away. He shifted in his chair slightly to rearrange the growing erection she had created. It seemed there was more to the queen than first thought, and the idea of seducing her and taking her to his bed had become something that he would do regardless of the personal cost. His aunt, the Duchess of Renn, sat on the opposite side of the queen, and began to question her regarding the food that would be served at one of her banquets. As Wynter was engaged, he turned his attention to his sister-in-law, Ashe.

"You're looking as beautiful as the first day you danced your way into my brother's heart, Lady Ashe. He is a lucky man to have you." Florian looked at the pretty woman with the pale blonde hair wound up in her customary bun and into her sparkling sapphire blue eyes. He held her gaze a moment longer than what most would deem appropriate, but he had discovered early on that it was a wonderful way to convey to women your want for them without saying a word. If someone caught you, or the woman was not inclined, it was also easy to brush off as a misunderstanding or that you weren't looking at them. "I hope he treats you as well as I would."

The peaches and cream reflection of the princess became flushed as she looked at Florian. "You always say the prettiest things."

"Only to the prettiest people."

Her laugh was high and light. "I can see why women always say yes to you."

"You have never said yes to me."

Ashe's blue eyes took on a different look for a moment, one that Florian couldn't read, before they cleared. "You have never asked."

Well, that certainly wasn't the answer I was expecting. Maybe they aren't as happy as they appear to the world. This was an insight he could exploit to get her into bed. "I didn't think I should ask."

Florian felt the light touch of Ashe's hand on his thigh as she leaned closer to him as if reaching for the meat on the platter that had been put in front of him. "A woman always wants to feel desired; you above all others should be aware of that. After all, I am sure it is in your bag of tricks." She took a slice of the ham with a large fork and squeezed his thigh before she returned to her normal, seated position and withdrew her hand.

His cock had gone from semi-hard from Wynter's directness to rock hard with Ashe's touch and hinted come-on. *Was it going to be this easy?* he wondered; until he caught a glance of his soon-to-be sister-in-law several seats down, on the other side of his parents, sitting primly and hanging onto every idiotic thing his brother said. He was going to have to put in some serious effort to get her where he wanted her. They had had a good beginning with the short conversation they had in the pavilion earlier today. He had put the thought into her head.

Several more courses came and went with him taking turns in subtly flirting with Wynter and Ashe. He was enjoying himself, but was also aware that they sat before everyone; he never wanted to show disrespect to either woman. This was a queen and a princess who would be a queen, and he had no desire to ruin their reputations; though, if he were honest, he would do it to win the challenge that had been laid before him. As the servants brought out trays laden with sugared fruits, clotted cream, filled fruit tarts, and other gloriously decadent desserts, Florian took a coin out of his pocket and began to roll it between his fingers in a trick that often caught people's attention.

"What do you have there?" asked Wynter as she watched the coin move across the top of his knuckles.

Florian moved back a little and kept the coin moving, backward and forwards.

"That's really clever, Florian," commented Ashe.

He kept watching the coin as if their words had not been precisely what he had been hoping to hear. "It is but a small coin, probably unimportant to everyone but me." He stopped his party trick and held the coin out to Queen Wynter. She took it and turned it over several times. He went on while she studied it. "When I was younger, I had difficulty sitting still at family dinners, and would often incur the wrath of my governess or father. My grandfather took out a coin one day and started playing with it, the flat gold circle flying across his knuckles as if it were magic. I was mesmerized and begged to be taught how to do it. No one said I couldn't learn at the dinner table, as grandfather was king at the time, so he began to teach me." He lowered his voice and allowed his emotions to get caught in his throat. "That coin is the most valuable thing I own. It holds such beautiful memories and brings me happiness."

Wynter handed the coin back to Florian, who then handed it over to Ashe who had held out her hand to see it. "That is a wonderful story." Wynter spoke gently, her tone a little less clipped. "I wish I could have met my grandparents. It must be wonderful to have something from the past that holds such happy thoughts. I have nothing like that."

It was Ashe that answered her. "I am so sorry to hear that. I have very little from my past as my stepmother and stepsisters wasted my father's money trying to get my Henri to take notice of them. I too wish I had something more of him to treasure." Ashe handed back the coin. "When we produce an heir, I hope you will take the time to teach your nephew that trick to keep him sitting quietly."

"I promise I will." He held up the coin a moment longer, keeping the women's attention on him. "So, neither of you have a special thing you would never part with for sentimental reasons?" He held his breath and hoped one of them took the bait.

Ashe looked over her shoulder at her husband then back at Florian and Wynter. "I do have my diamond slippers. If I had to choose something I valued above all other material things, it would be those. They did catch me a prince, after all."

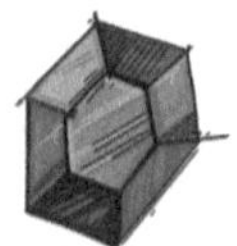

Florian awoke the next morning pleased with yesterday's progress, but also aware that the person he felt would be the most difficult to seduce in the time frame given he had not interacted with at the dinner.

He was up and dressed before his manservant had entered his royal suite to wake him. Tumas raised an eyebrow but said nothing at the unusual situation. Typically, Tumas had the unfortunate task of escorting whatever young, and sometimes not so young, woman the prince had slept with the night prior out of the suite, and on occasion, smuggle them out to keep their reputation intact.

"I will be joining my family for breakfast this morning. I will bathe when I return."

Tumas's eyebrows disappeared entirely into his hairline at that statement, but he refrained from saying anything his eyebrows did not already convey.

Florian hid his amusement at the response, and hummed to himself as he straightened his collar in the burnished full-length mirror that stood in the corner of his room, and ran a hand over his short, spiky dark brown hair. He made the decision to leave the strings to his linen shirt undone for a more relaxed look, and to show off his tanned, smooth pecs. After all, it was breakfast with his family and a little informality wouldn't go astray if either Dawn or Ashe were there.

"I shan't be long," he called over his shoulder as he left his suite. Pausing for a second, he allowed his bodyguards, who would have assumed that he would not be emerging for at least another candlemark, to gather themselves and fall in line behind him.

The humming continued as he walked down the family wing of the palace and entered the private dining room of the King and Queen of the Kingdom of Dreams. Everyone stopped speaking as he walked toward his mother and kissed her cheek, moved to Ashe to peck her cheek, and then walked around to the other side of the table to kiss Dawn's cheek too. It was a calculated move to get both women further used to his proximity. He nodded in greeting to his father and brothers before walking to the serving board that sat to the side of the room. It held simple fare, as the family always ate a smaller meal in the morning as it was expected of them to eat larger, more elaborate meals throughout the day and when they had guests. He took no notice of a page who was sent scurrying to the kitchen to collect a plate and cutlery for the unexpected arrival of the young prince; though, Florian did deliberately take longer than was necessary to choose his food to give the young boy a chance to return and set a place at the table.

In no time, the prince was seated next to Phillip, whom he liked least out of his two brothers, and was slowly eating his eggs as his family returned to discussing the day's formalities. "The hounds and horses have been chosen and will be ready to hunt by midmorning as planned," announced Henri as he took a slice of cheese and added it to a slice of apple.

"Well done, son." The king congratulated his firstborn. He looked at his other two sons, who neither truly enjoyed the hunt as much as their father and brother. "Will either of you be joining us today?"

Phillip shook his head and swallowed the cider he had just sipped. "I promised Dawn that I would escort her around the Citizens' Fair today. I know you will make an appearance later, but she wants to meet the people, do some shopping, and maybe join in some street games." He smiled at his betrothed, and Florian tried to figure out if it was genuine or whether he had agreed to all the frivolity to avoid hunting with their brother. The king and Henri had nothing to say to that; there was no answer when a dragon-killer refused to go hunting, as he had nothing to prove.

Damn, Florian swore to himself as their eyes now turned to him. He picked up a sweet roll and took a bite so he had time to think. *Maybe coming to breakfast hadn't been the best idea after all. I haven't even had a chance to speak to either woman, and now, I need a good excuse to get out of hunting.*

"Ashe and I were also considering heading out to see the fair today." Florian's mother spoke softly, her light hazel eyes crinkled as she smiled at him. "Perhaps you could accompany us, Florian? It would be unseemly for the princess and me to be seen without a proper male of the royal line. And I think no one need question your hunting prowess after you showed everyone what you can do with a bow yesterday."

Florian almost laughed aloud at his mother's statement. She had always done what she wanted, when she wanted—within the confines of her role—and if she wanted to wander through a fair full of the citizens of the capital without a male escort then she would. She, as always, was giving him an out, and he lept on it.

"I would be honored to walk the fair with you and Lady Ashe. Father and Henri can join us in the royal pavilion for afternoon tea, perhaps?"

Though Florian knew his father would have preferred him to join the hunt, he would also be relieved that Florian had agreed to go to the fair so the King didn't have to. He didn't have the gift of easy speech that Florian and the queen did, so sometimes struggled to make small talk with anyone outside of the nobility. Henri would be thrilled to monopolize their father's time and show off his hunting skills now that Phillip wouldn't be joining them.

Thanks to his mother, not only was Florian saved from killing animals for no other reason than because they could, he would also now have the chance to spend several hours with Ashe.

Glorious smells filled the streets as large spits that held boar were slowly turned over hot coals by men holding sharp knives who sliced off thin, succulent pieces for anyone who asked, all provided for from the coffers of the royal family. No one in the capital would go hungry today. Vendors hawked their wares loudly, the sounds competing with the laughter of children who delighted at tumblers and strong men competitions on street corners. The Citizens' Fair was in full swing, and Florian was enjoying himself immensely.

The queen and the princess browsed ribbon stalls and rug makers, as well as woodworkers and soap makers. They both took their time and chatted with any citizen who stopped to bow or curtsy and offer their congratulations and thanks for the generosity the royal family was showing this day.

Florian picked a length of blue ribbon, the smooth shiny material reminding him of Queen Dawn's gown. The one she had been wearing when his brother Phillip had come to her rescue and kissed her awake. The picture of her, her lips parted slightly, her breast rising and falling with each breath as she slept would haunt him forever. He had fantasized several times about lifting that perfect blue dress to find out whether she was just as perfect underneath. Florian ran the ribbon through his fingers once more before a thought came to him. "How much for the ribbon?" he asked the skinny, hawk-nosed stall owner.

"The prince can have it as a gift," he answered, bowing deeply.

"That is a most generous offer, but I insist on paying you for it." Florian chose not to haggle with the man, he simply waved his hand and the bursar who had been sent to carry the coin purse for the queen and princess stepped forward and paid the man a generous amount of money for a simple ribbon. Florian spooled the ribbon around his fingers before carefully placing it in his tunic pocket.

Princess Ashe had finished speaking with an elderly couple at the front of the stall, and had moved deeper into the shop where the ribbon seller had a small amount of embroidered kerchiefs pegged along a line. The queen was talking to a mother and her two small children; the palace guards stopped anyone else from coming close and they blocked the entrance to the stall. The stall owner hovered near the queen. Florian casually made his way toward Ashe and came to stand beside her. He reached up and gently held the kerchief next to the one Ashe was admiring. "Very good needlework," he said conversationally.

"I used to sit by my attic window and embroider while I dreamed of being rescued by a handsome prince." Ashe let the kerchief slide between her fingers. "My needlework is not as fine as this craftsmanship," she noted.

"And how do you like the rescuing? Has it been everything you wished for?" Florian asked lightly, keeping his expression friendly.

"In some ways, it was everything I hoped, but like everything, our imaginations never see the reality of the whole situation, just the pretty things."

Florian was surprised at the answer. He had expected her to say she was deliriously happy, not to be honest that there were parts that were unexpected and perhaps not wonderful. He unpegged the kerchief she had been admiring and handed it to her, their fingers brushing. He felt his skin tingle and relished the feeling. It was always the same when he courted a woman; that feeling of building anticipation. That longing that grew in your gut, the need to be near them, to consume them is what he loved about pursuing women. It was there with Ashe now it had been suggested, and he would feel the heat rise until he had her. He noted that she didn't pull away as their fingers touched. He looked into her sapphire blue eyes and saw interest. Ashe licked her perfect lips, and Florian smiled knowingly.

They were interrupted by the shop owner who saw Ashe holding the kerchief. "Do you like my wife's fine work, Princess?"

"I do. She has a delicate touch with such fine needlework."

"I would like to buy the kerchief." Florian spoke to the vendor.

"As you wish, Prince Florian. I will go and haggle with the coin purse holder." He bowed away from the pair.

Ashe turned to Florian. "That was kind of you, but I am not sure entirely appropriate."

Florian shrugged. "I am all for inappropriate." He gave her a meaningful look before going on. "Besides, I bought a small gift for my soon-to-be sister-in-law, I can certainly buy one for my already sister-in-law."

The gorgeous woman rested her hand on his forearm and looked into his hazel eyes. "Thank you. I will have to find an appropriate gift for you now."

"I am sure you will come up with something suitable." He smiled at her, all innocence.

By the time the queen, princess, and Florian arrived at the huge canopy that stood in the center of the fair, the nobles were merrily singing along to a bard that had been invited to play for them. The canopy housed the royal family and invited guests, and it was obvious from the loud, raucous singing that the ale had been flowing since midday. As the trio was greeted with unsteady curtsies and bows, Florian smiled indulgently as several people who had not had the chance to congratulate him for his win yesterday took the opportunity to do so. He was handed a large tankard of mead and clinked cups with his father. "How did the hunt go?"

"Splendidly. How did the shopping go? Could you curb your mother's spending?"

"Alas, no. She is quite skilled at negotiating prices though. She haggled with the best of them."

"Between you and me, I think she enjoys it."

"I am sure she does," agreed Florian. He looked around at the mingling guests. "Everyone seems to be enjoying themselves."

Further talk was impossible as everyone started to applaud a juggler as he began to toss heavy swords in the air. The queen came over and kissed her husband on the cheek in greeting. Florian took the moment to slip away from his parents and mingle amongst the guests. He circulated, but in reality, he was searching for a particular person. He found her engaged in conversation with the Viscount George and his nephew Pierre.

Florian watched her laugh freely, her chin-length, dark hair held back with a simple beaten metal band swung as she tilted her head to one side. She was ethereal and earthy all at once, and he longed to touch her. There was a spark of attraction and heat he hadn't experienced before, and he found it intoxicating. She wore a simple dress, but in a rich red fabric that reminded him of apples. He watched

Wynter respond to what had been said, and both the older and younger noblemen laughed with her.

It was as if something pulled him toward her, as if he had no control over his actions. He found his legs moving before his brain had caught up. Trying not to panic, he approached the group. He was typically in control and already planning his next move, but for some reason after last night's dinner he was a little unsure of himself. She had been witty and interested, but also a tad brusque and guarded in a different manner than any other woman he had dealt with. Though, if he were honest, he usually only chose women that he knew would be interested in him. Dawn and Ashe had been more receptive to his flirting. Wynter had appeared at ease with it, but he was uncertain, and uncertainty was a new sensation for him to experience when it came to women. One he didn't enjoy at all.

Florian plastered a smile on his face and told himself she was just like any other woman...and he had had them all. Perhaps, Dawn was not going to be the most difficult.

All three turned to greet him as he approached. The Viscount and his nephew bowed while Wynter inclined her head. Florian bowed deeply to the queen while nodding acknowledgment to the two gentlemen. "We were just discussing the successful hunt this morning." Wynter spoke in her clipped tone. "Pierre was exceptional."

"That is kind of Your Majesty to say." The young man blushed.

An odd feeling settled into Florian's gut; though, he couldn't recognize what it was. "Marvelous to hear." He smiled at Pierre.

"I was surprised you didn't attend today's hunt," commented the Viscount.

"It's not really my thing." He winked at the old man. "And it would not do to show my brother up two days in a row."

All three laughed at his jest and Florian's strange emotions from before began to dissipate. He was back to his usual, charming self. "Did you ride with the hunt, Your Majesty?" he asked Wynter as some of the noblewomen occasionally chose to ride out with the men; though, they never actually got involved with the hunting section of the day.

"Yes, it was a lovely day for it. Thankfully, not as hot as yesterday." She smiled up at him, her pretty eyes drawing him in. "Though, I do enjoy the heat." Her eyes lingered on his a little longer than was proper for a queen before they swung back to Pierre, who had stopped a passing servant carrying drinks on a tray.

The servant offered drinks to everyone, and they all accepted with thanks. "If you weren't out hunting, am I permitted to ask how you spent the morning, Prince Florian?" Viscount George asked jovially.

"Of course. I was with my mother and Princess Ashe, wandering the fair and markets to engage with our citizens. I have had quite a wonderful time watching minstrels, shopping for trinkets, and even got beaten by a lad in a pie-eating contest. I also had to pull mother away from a sleight-of-hand artist as he kept losing, and that was ruining everyone's fun."

Pierre frowned as if not quite understanding. Florian noticed and so did Wynter, who saved the young man from having to ask by simply saying, "The poor guy. Probably one of his biggest days with all those people out with money to spend and willing to try their luck against him and along comes the queen and he has to lose to her—it wouldn't be right to take her money."

Florian spent the next half a candlemark chatting with the queen and others as they stopped by to be seen talking to her. Some were genuine, some were not, but she was pleasant to all. It was only when Phillip and Dawn came up to speak to Wynter did Florian excuse himself from the conversation.

This sort of event was usually something Florian enjoyed. Mingling, drinking, flirting with the beautiful women who attended, and watching troubadours and contortionists was always entertaining. Today was different. He was too concerned with winning the challenge that had been issued to truly enjoy anything. He couldn't flirt with any of them as there were too many people around to risk being overheard. He decided it was time to take his leave and return to the palace.

Florian found Tumas on the outskirts of the oversized canopy, chatting with several other trusted servants, who technically weren't on duty, but had chosen to stay close to their employer in case they were needed. "Tumas, a word?"

Tumas nodded and followed Florian out into the late afternoon sunlight. "I am heading back to the palace." The prince took out a small coin purse and pressed it into his manservant's hand. "Go, enjoy yourself. I don't expect to see you till tomorrow morning and you better be nursing a hangover."

"That is most generous, Your Highness."

Florian smiled at him. "With what you do for me it is barely enough."

"Let me organize your horse and guards and send you on your way."

"Would you be so kind as to take care of mine too, Tumas?" a lovely, gentle voice spoke from behind Florian.

"Of course, Princess." Tumas walked briskly toward several footmen who were taking care of the horses of the nobles that were picketed nearby.

Florian turned to find Ashe standing near him. "Returning to the palace so soon?"

"I need a little space from all these people. Henri is busy and looks like he will be for several more candlemarks, so I thought I would head back and take a short nap and refresh myself before coming back to join him for supper."

"I was planning on doing something similar," Florian said. He looked at her and said quietly under his breath, "though, napping is not what I had in mind."

Princess Ashe flushed, but she did not look away; instead, she laughed lightly, her gorgeous eyes growing wide before turning and waiting for Tumas to come with the horses and honor guard.

"Here we are," Florian announced as they arrived at Ashe and Henri's suite. "Get some rest." He opened the door. "I will perhaps see you at supper later." Florian stepped inside and held the heavy door open for her. He looked around the outer room of the suite and noted the diamond slippers that had allowed his brother to find his beloved. They sat sparkling in the late afternoon sun, upon a pedal stool and enclosed in a square glass box.

Ashe hovered at the entrance to the room while he stood there waiting for her to enter. He nodded toward the case. "Is it really safe to have those there?" She followed his gaze to the shoes that threw colored light across the room.

"You sound like Henri. I love them and they remind me to be grateful for all I have learned and gained."

"So, they would be the most important thing that you own?" Florian asked casually, he looked around the rest of the room, taking in where everything lay.

"Oh, most assuredly."

A tiny thrill ran up Florian's spine as he gained another little win toward the prize he had wagered for with Stic. She had said as much last night, but a little confirmation hurt no one. "I can't stand and hold the door all day, Your Highness. I need to attend to the matters I spoke of," he prompted in the hope she would enter the room and reveal her hand.

Ashe looked down either side of the corridor and then nodded as if making up her mind. She stepped through the door, and he leaned in to kiss her on the cheek. "Take care." Florian pretended to move to walk out.

"Wait," she said quietly, her hand reached for his forearm.

Keeping his face neutral, the prince closed the door and turned to face the always impeccably groomed woman. What he wouldn't do to see her disheveled and bent over before him. He let his eyes travel from where he noted her hand on his arm, up to her face, and he allowed the want he felt at that moment to reflect in his eyes. "Don't tease me, Ashe."

She bit her lower lip and fluttered her eyelashes at him. "I have a slight dilemma."

"Something I can help you with?"

Ashe continued to hold onto his arm. "I let all of our personal servants have the day off..." Her voice trailed into silence.

It took Florian only an instant to understand what she was implying. "I am certain you can find a maid that will help you."

"Yes, I am certain I could, and I am positive that is what I will tell Henri what happened."

"But that is not what is going to happen?" He feigned innocence. "How will you ever get out of that dress?"

"Florian, we both know how I am going to get out of this dress."

He raised his brows at her. "I will need my arm back." She released his arm. "Turn around."

Ashe gave him one final look and turned her back to him. Florian scrutinized the tightly laced bodice. His finger traced one of the ribbons to find the end. As he tugged on the lacing, he bent forward and breathed on her exposed neck, as her golden hair was up in its customary bun. She shivered at the unexpected, exhaled breath. "You have a glorious neck," he breathed out as he said the words. "No wonder you wear your hair up so frequently." Florian's hands continued to work at loosening the ribbons that held her bodice in place.

He licked his lips as he bent down and then placed a tender kiss where her shoulder and neck joined. Ashe sighed and moved her head to the other side, exposing her neck further and clearly inviting him to continue kissing her. With soft butterfly kisses, he trailed his lips up her neck until he took her earlobe into his mouth. Florian's hands continued to work the lace loose enough so he could lift the bodice above her head. Ashe lifted her arms to help him get the piece of clothing off. "Lock the door," she ordered as she reached around to the back of her waist and began to untie the now exposed strings that held her blue over-skirt and petticoats in place.

Florian did what he was told and moved to lock the door. He aimed to seduce his sister-in-law and steal her shoes; not get caught and ruin her marriage, and hurt his brother. He would follow the challenge through, but he would try to avoid causing irreversible damage. He watched Ashe struggle with her ties for a moment, the rays of light from her diamond slippers danced across her shoulders and face and he took in the beauty of the woman before him. Her pointed chin and high cheekbones blended perfectly with her lightly puckered lips and wide eyes. He grew hard as he thought about letting her hair down and winding it around his fist to hold her in place as he pounded into her.

"Are you going to gawk or help?" Ashe asked him as she dropped her arms to her sides.

"I was admiring you." He came to stand before her. He reached up and began to pull the pins from her hair. He didn't know why it was essential for him to see her hair down, but it had become almost an obsession. As he took out the last pin her hair tumbled down.

Ashe shook her head and her hair settled around her shoulders and down her back, reaching her waist. Florian ran his fingers through her hair, feeling the silky tresses slide over his knuckles. He brought it up to his face and inhaled. Roses. Luxurious, sweet, and inviting. He let her hair fall and put one hand to her waist, while the other reached up and moved to the nape of her neck, where he fisted her hair and pulled her to him. He crushed his lips against hers. His tongue danced with hers as she matched his fervor. Without breaking the kiss, he released her hair and finished untying her skirts with practiced ease. They fell to the floor in a pool of fabric.

Her hands began to remove his coat and he helped by shrugging out of it. Florian broke the passionate kiss to pull his long-sleeved shirt over his head. They both panted and watched each other as they finished undressing. Her ragged breath a further turn on. He noted there was no hesitation as she pulled off her breaches and unlaced her corset. He followed suit by pulling off his pants.

They both stood there breathing heavily, Ashe's body was fine and surprisingly lightly muscled. Florian guessed it was from all the hard work she had done for her stepmother for all of those years. He held out his hand and she took it; he noted her hand was steady. Ashe stepped out of the large pile of clothes around her feet. Florian led her to a velvet divan with a large, curved side and no back. He pushed her down onto the long seat, moving her so her back was leaning against the curved side and her legs lying along the length of the divan.

"You are breathtaking." He trailed his fingers lightly across her parted lips and down her throat, tracing a collarbone before continuing down over her sternum and swirling around her belly button. He walked his fingers over her mound and watched with satisfaction as she arched her back and opened her legs for him to explore further. Florian let his hand rest there as he knelt on the plush rug.

A slow smile slid over his face as he brought his head down to her pert, small breast. Florian sucked it into his mouth and her nipple grew hard. He nipped it with his teeth, eliciting a soft moan from Ashe. As he continued to suck and twirl his tongue around her nipple he moved his hand further down. His fingers found her clit and moved in a firm, circular motion for several moments before continuing over her slick folds and finding her opening. She groaned louder as he pushed one finger into her, slowly moving it in and out. Florian's core tightened as his hand became coated with her and he pushed a second finger inside, the warmth of her closing around him.

Ashe arched her back further, pushing her breast up and he bit her harder. He let go of her nipple and planted kisses up her neck and eventually found her mouth, where he was passionately greeted. As he moved in and out, he curled his fingers slightly, rubbing along the rough spot that he had discovered could send a woman into a panting mess, especially when combined with what he was about to do. As their tongues fought and their lips begged for connection, Florian continued moving his fingers but also stretched his thumb up to find Ashe's clit. She ground her hips against his hand as he slowly moved his thumb in a circular motion. Feeling her writhe beneath him made Florian's cock demand attention, but he put it off, enjoying the sensation of pleasuring this beautiful woman.

Whimpers and groans filled the tastefully decorated room as Florian built Ashe to her first orgasm. He pulled his head back, breaking the kiss as he applied firmer pressure to her clit, moving from side to side in the tiniest motion that would make her come—hard. He watched her face. Her eyes were closed and her mouth was wide, while her chest rose and fell quickly with her heavy panting. Suddenly, she stilled as if time had stopped, and he knew that she was falling. He felt her clamp around his fingers in waves and he continued to slowly move in and out until she sighed and slumped back against the divan.

He withdrew his hand and wiped her on his hard cock. Slowly moving his hand up and down as he stood and moved to the end of the divan. He let go of himself and knelt between her parted legs, slowly crawling his way up, kissing her tenderly along her inner thigh as he did.

Ashe brought her head up from where it rested on the arched wing of the velvet-covered lounge and watched him with hungry eyes. She licked her lips, catching her bottom lip between her teeth for several moments. Florian winked at her as he continued to lay tiny kisses along the curve of her thigh and up her flat stomach. He paused as he reached her breasts. Taking the hard, perfect nipple into his mouth while rolling the other one between his fingers and pinching it until she moaned. Freeing her nipples, he continued to slide up her body, his torso grazing hers as his lips found hers and his cocked halted at her entrance. He kissed her passionately, his mouth devouring hers, his want growing to a level he could no longer deny, and he slowly pushed against her. He slid in easily and halted for a moment before pulling out and pushing in again with a little more force. He repeated this several more times, her hips rising to meet him, and drawing him in deeper.

Florian held himself still as he filled her fully, she sheathed him, and it was glorious. Ashe continued to kiss him, her arms around his neck, keeping him locked to her lips. He felt her release one hand and slid it down his back, her fingernails lightly running over his shoulder blades. Her hand came to rest on his ass, and she grabbed it firmly, pushing him those few more inches and gyrating her hips.

He pulled his head back from her and watched as he withdrew until only the tip of his cock rested in her. Florian thrust firmly and deeply, repeating the pattern again and again. He felt his pleasure build and held onto the fine edge of riding the wave of sensations but not taking it too far and toppling over the crest. He slowly withdrew and kissed her quickly. "Turn around."

Ashe frowned at him for a moment. "Okay," she complied.

Florian sat back on his feet while Ashe moved her legs and turned her body to face the other way. She rested her hands on the highest part of the winged section. Florian grabbed his cock and pumped his hand up and down several times as he watched her kneel before him, her gorgeous ass on display, and her opening glistening and waiting for him. Letting go of himself he took hold of her hips and eased himself into her, allowing her to get used to the feeling. Ashe moaned and pushed back into him. With growing need and his core a flame, he withdrew as he whispered, "Ready?"

He watched her flex her hands on the velvet fabric. "Yes."

And with those consenting words, he thrust deep, deeper than he could be in any other position. Hard and fast, in and out. He wound his hand around her hair and tugged on the ponytail, making her head come back. His stomach muscles tightened as he slammed into her, over and over, his orgasm building back up. She was glorious as she moaned out his name, making him pump faster. He held onto her hair, but let go of her hip, moving his hand to find her clit and build her up so they fell together, each pulling the other along. With practiced fingers he circled faster, applying more pressure. Knowing the friction of his cock inside and his fingers working on her would bring her to orgasm quickly.

Florian couldn't fight it any longer and let go of his control, slamming into her and pumping out his seed at the same moment as she clenched around him, drawing out his pleasure and hers. He groaned loudly and bent over her back, burying his face in her beautiful hair as they both stilled and the room became quiet.

Princess Ashe

"Florian?" Ashe picked up the abandoned dress and held it against her nakedness as if modesty was needed. It was silly, but she didn't want him to see her exposed now their passion had ebbed.

He paused in his struggle to get his tunic over his head. "Yes?"

"Why now?"

"Sorry, what do you mean?"

"I have been married to your brother for two years. Why all of a sudden did you want to bed me?" She watched his stomach muscles ripple as he pulled the tunic over them. He truly was delicious. Henri was handsome in a clean, wholesome way, his body strong and solid and his love-making rarely varied in position or setting. Florian was handsome in a sexy, I will make you pant and beg, kind of way, his body sculptured and leaner and he didn't make love, he seduced and fucked. Nothing had changed by her sleeping with Florian; she still loved Henri with all of her heart and welcomed the idea of spending the rest of her life with him. Yet, now she knew what could go on in the bed chamber and she was going to try to introduce a little more of it to Henri.

Florian yanked on his boots and straightened his clothing as he stood up. He ran his hand over his close-cropped, brown hair and watched her with those laughing hazel eyes for several moments. He didn't speak.

"I was warned of your reputation as soon as I began to live here. And will admit have always been a little disap-pointed that you never bothered to try. I thought perhaps I wasn't your type."

She watched his tongue ran across his lips and a fire blazed within her as she recalled what a simple tongue could do. "You are beautiful, and you were broken when you came to live here," he finally answered. "You were nervous around me, and Henri was insanely protective."

Ashe thought about his words. They were all true. She had been broken from the abuse suffered at the hands of her stepmother and stepsisters. It had taken her a long time to heal from those years. Henri had been overprotective at times and had been attentive to her every want. It had been wonderful at first but then had become claustrophobic. Thankfully, once she had spoken to him about it, he had given her space. "I am not nervous anymore."

He grinned that wicked smile that she had watched ensnare many a woman. "I noticed."

Ashe couldn't help it as she laughed. "You are bad."

"Who warned you about me?"

It was her turn to give him an evil grin. "Everyone."

Florian shrugged. "I shouldn't really be surprised. Answer me this: why when I flirted with you did you respond?"

She arched an eyebrow at him. "Your talents are talked about amongst the servants, and I wanted first-hand knowledge. Your brother is my first and only love, but I wanted to experience one other man, and I considered you the best choice for many reasons."

Ashe finally noted the sun had set and realized that someone would probably be sent to check on her soon. "So, tell me, Prince Florian, how do you get a suitor to leave once you are done?"

"Usually not quite that directly, but yes, it is probably wise for me to go. I do believe that it best if you leave the room before I open the door just in case guards or anyone else is walking by." He looked her up and down and she tried to ignore the suggestion that sweeping gaze held. "We can't have you naked, but for a crumpled dress pressed against you, being seen by anyone. I will wait here and once you have gone into your bedchamber I will open the door and leave. If anyone is there to witness it I will say I stopped by to check on you as I was the one who had brought you back because you were feeling poorly."

"I see you have done this type of thing before. I am uncertain if we shall ever do this again, so I will say thank you and goodbye."

Florian bowed deeply to her, and she knew that he meant the respect he was showing. He was a difficult man to understand sometimes. A cad who was considerate and kind.

It was only when she went to turn to leave the room did she consider her bottom would be on display as she exited the room. It was a silly thing to worry about, so in the end, she stood a little straighter, and just for good measure, she swung her hips a little more than normal as she left the room without any further words. Her exit was followed by a soft whistle, and she had a tiny chuckle to herself as she closed the door firmly behind her. Ashe moved to her private dressing room and closed the door. No one would bother her in here, even Henri. She bundled her dress up and lay down on the richly carpeted floor, placing the make-shift cushion under her hips and bottom. Ashe raised her legs and placed them on the door, essentially barring anyone from barging in and finding her in such an odd position.

Ashe let her mind wander as she lay there, her legs raised and her pelvis elevated, her hands placed protectively over her lower stomach. "Work," she whispered into the cool air of the sumptuously appointed room.

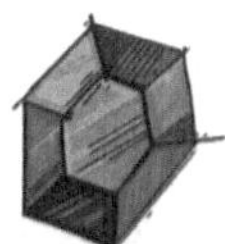

The music swelled as it reached its crescendo and the dancers twirled their partners one last time as the sound of the stringed instruments faded. Florian was enjoying himself and had congratulated his mother as the ballroom looked sensational with its bright bunting and hundreds of candles, rather than the lanterns and torches that usually lit the room. The candles cast a softer glow and there was less smoke hanging in the air. Men looked dashing in their finest suits and the women looked beautiful in their large, striking gowns and sparkling jewels.

The evening had been interesting thus far, with Wynter seemingly slightly more open to his flirting and Dawn meeting his gaze several times. Ashe had been exceptionally friendly toward him and he had the suspicion that she would be happy to meet for another encounter. He wasn't certain how he felt about that. He wanted to win the challenge and claim his prize, but sleeping with his brother's wife just for the sheer fun of it was different from doing it for a reason.

"How goes the challenge?" Stic asked before he popped another grape into his generous mouth. "My guess is you have succeeded with your sister-in-law."

"What makes you say that?"

Stic raised his pale eyebrows at the prince. "I think I have proven before that there is not much I don't know."

"Wish you would tell me how you do it."

"You know you have to earn that privilege."

Florian felt the all too familiar frustration rise at this ongoing conversation between them then dissipate. He would sleep with the three women of Stic's choosing and steal their most prized possessions to present to Stic and then Florian would finally discover his friend's secret.

Stic popped another grape in his mouth and grinned at his friend. "I look forward to claiming you, or should I say my prize?"

Florian had always been aware of Stic's preference for men, and once when they had been absurdly drunk Stic had tried to kiss his friend. That was when the first discussion of an outrageous challenge that would result in one of them getting what they wanted most from the other had first been proposed. Yet, every time a dare had been issued one of them had always claimed that it wasn't big enough for the ultimate reward to be given so it had never been decided who the winner would be. Until now. The thought of finally knowing Stic's secret ways was worth just about anything to Florian, and if he wrecked a few relationships in the process, did it matter? He was determined to uncover the truth. It didn't cross his mind what he would do if he lost and had to go to bed with Stic.

Queen Dawn was slowly making her way around the

crowded dance floor, several palace guards and her lady-in-waiting trailing respectfully behind. She was getting closer to Florian, and he saw his chance. Turning and handing his empty goblet to his friend, he smirked at Stic. "Here, hold this. I have a task to finish."

Raising the empty goblet in salute, Stic simply smiled at the comment.

As Florian moved toward the queen, he took in how radiant she was in her deep pink ball gown. The dress was similar to the blue one she had been wearing when he and Phillip had discovered her asleep in the old, decrepit castle, guarded by a few old men who had been the sons and grandsons of the original guards when she had pricked her finger and been cursed to sleep. Her golden, softly curled tresses flowed down her back and her eyes sparkled as she greeted those who greeted her. Dawn was only new to being a queen, but she already conducted herself impeccably.

"Your Majesty, may I have the honor of the next dance?" he asked as he walked up to her.

"Why, of course, Prince Florian. It would be a pleasure."

They waited in silence, watching the current dancers complete the waltz and applaud the orchestra before some moved away from the dance floor, while others escorted their partners into the designated dance space. Florian held out his arm and Dawn took it. The slight pressure of her touch was enough to wake up his libido and send a shiver down his spine.

Florian held out his arms and Dawn stepped into them as he closed them around her. He held her lightly, allowing her to feel that she could leave at any moment. He wanted her to be aware that this was a choice.

The music started and he felt a slight tremble in her warm, fine hand as they began to move around the floor. "Are you nervous to be with me?" he asked.

"Just nervous," she answered quietly. "I still occasionally struggle with everyone scrutinizing my every move, and I am not sure my dancing is up to the challenge of stopping any gossip of how terrible it is."

This was perfect for Florian, who had been forced to take dance lessons for years. "You need to relax and trust me. I will not let you look anything other than competent, but I am going to have to hold you a little firmer to get you to go where I want you to. Is that okay?"

Dawn smiled gratefully at him. "More than okay." She gripped his hand tighter to prove that she was willing to comply.

Florian flattened his hand against her lower back and moved her around the floor a little more. After a few moments, he felt her body relax and she became far easier to lead.

He smiled reassuringly at her and then looked further up at the heavy crown that rested on her head. "Does that ever get too much?"

"It can give me a headache, but I think it is worth it. It is a clear declaration of who I am, but also reminds everyone of what I have lost."

Her answer was unusually direct, which urged him to ask, "Did you think any more on my question?" He stepped closer as the dance dictated he should. They circled each other, their hands clasped in the center.

"What question?" she asked sweetly. Obviously now more comfortable with him and on the dance floor.

"Not buying it. You know what question." They dropped their hands and stepped out and then back in before his hand slid back around her tiny waist while the other took her hand.

She looked up at him for a second and then looked away. "Do I wish it had been you that had kissed me awake and slain the wicked enchantress who had cursed me?" Dawn twirled under his arm before returning to her position and continuing the conversation. "No. Phillip will make a wonderful Prince-Consort; he is supportive, brave, and smart. Something I will need as I fight to bring my country back together after one hundred years of no true monarch."

Florian's stomach dropped. That was not the answer he wanted to hear. Had he pushed her too quickly to make a decision? Perhaps, he had grown too sure of himself because she had relaxed with him while they danced. If only he had more time. He felt his triumphant win slip a little away from his reach...and tried not to think about what it would be like to kiss Stic.

"Have I ever thought about kissing you?" The music died and she let go of his hand. Stepping away and nodding her head as a thank you. She didn't curtsy like everyone else; she was a queen.

He bowed and waited for her to answer her own question. As she opened her mouth to speak, Phillip appeared behind her. Florian smiled pleasantly as he approached. Phillip put his hand around Dawn's waist, where Florian's had been only moments before. It was clear he was claiming her. "Would you care to dance with me now? You always say you are a terrible dancer, but you looked completely comfortable out there."

Dawn put her hand over Phillip's but looked directly at Florian as she answered. "Yes. I would like that."

The couple twirled away, leaving Florian to ponder if he had read too much into that last statement or whether it meant what he thought it had implied. He moved out of the way of the dancing couples and made his way to a large punch bowl where he was offered a glass of the sweet juice and wine mixture his mother had grown so fond of. He took the proffered drink and sipped on it as he thought about his next move. Had she meant yes, she had thought about what it would be like to kiss him? Or was he just hoping that is what she was implying?

"You dance well," a strong, feminine voice said beside him.

He turned his head to find Queen Wynter standing to his right. "Would you care to join me on the dance floor? I do enjoy dancing; it allows me to hold pretty women."

The Queen of the Fourth Kingdom laughed in a rich, deep tone that made Florian's core flutter. "Maybe later." She turned him down and he shrugged as if he hadn't thought about holding her close to him. "I wanted to ask you about several artworks that I saw on my way here. Would you like to give me a tour?"

His ego soared at the chance to talk to her alone. "Of course, Your Majesty. I am here to serve you." He offered her his arm.

The shiny red apple sat in the center of the fruit bowl, the dappled sunlight playing along its surface. The painting was a perfect replica of the fruit and bowl, but Florian had never truly seen the point of this type of painting. "It reminds me of another apple..." Queen Wynter murmured, and Florian wondered if she was speaking to herself.

"There have been rumors that the former Queen of the Fourth Kingdom poisoned you with an apple," he admitted, thinking she must know what the gossip is about her.

"Yes, and no. The rumors are half true. She did poison me, but it was a ruby in the shape of an apple."

"I would like to hear your tale sometime. It was quite the scandal that you declined a prince." He raised an eyebrow at her. "I mean, who does that?"

"I am sure you wouldn't know. Does anyone ever say no to you?" she asked, a smile playing across her lovely features.

"The night is young, it could happen," he joked.

They began to walk again, further down the corridor and away from the noise of the ball. Her one personal bodyguard and his own guard had been left near the beginning of the corridor and it was wonderful to have her alone, without worrying about what people could overhear. "Was there any other painting, in particular, you wanted to see?"

"There is an odd one just up ahead that you could tell me about."

Florian tried to remember what the next few paintings were. He walked these halls so frequently but rarely took note of his surroundings. They walked by several battle scenes which Wynter barely looked at. She stopped when they got to a smaller painting next to an alcove that was empty but usually housed a large, bronze statue of a horse. Under the small painting was a half-circle table that held a large, white vase filled with bright fuchsias. The horse statue that usually stood in the alcove and the table, which always contained large bouquets of colorful flowers, drew your eyes away from the small painting that hung near it.

"Care to explain that?" the queen gestured to the canvas.

Florian looked up and began to chuckle; he had forgotten this small anomaly and it made him laugh to discover it still hung in the palace halls. "That is a frying pan, Your Majesty."

"I know what it is. what I want to know is why you have a painting of it?"

"It is a family in-joke. They apparently make amazing weapons."

Her gorgeous brown eyes filled with mirth, "Well, yes, I guess they would make a great weapon if you had nothing else at hand." She turned to the empty alcove; it was filled with shadows as this area of the corridor was dimly lit for there was no need for anyone to be down there tonight. "And what is usually here?"

Florian stepped closer to the alcove, brushing by her and inhaling her scent. His hand rested lightly on her back as he moved her an inch or two to the side so he could look better at the area. "A statue of a horse reared up on its hind legs. If I recall correctly, the horse has something to do with the frying pan-wielding relative. We can always ask if you really want to know. The details are fuzzy now, but I loved the story when I was a child."

"I think I do want to know at some point."

She was so close to him, their arms brushed as she moved to peer into the alcove, and he reigned in his instinct to say something suggestive. "Your Majesty," he began, his words uttered softly in the quiet of the empty corridor. Music drifted toward them, but it wasn't enough to cover their conversation if they spoke too loudly. His nervousness at being around her returned.

"Yes, Your Highness?"

He held up a flower that he had plucked from the vase. "Please, call me Florian." He looked down at her, and licked his lips as he watched hers spread into a smile.

"I thought I might call you Prince Charming; after all, that's what the ladies of the court tell me you are." Her smile turned into a wicked grin as she took the fuchsia from him.

He took a step closer to her, his back to the alcove, so she knew she wasn't blocked in and could move away from him if she chose. "Really? And what else do the ladies of the court say?" He was back in his comfort area of flirting.

"Many things." She didn't go on, but her eyes glinted with mischief.

"And do you believe what you have been told, Your Majesty?" He inched a little closer, his groin tingling as his core tightened.

Wynter took a step closer, her breasts only inches from his chest, her hot breath landing on his neck. "Call me Wynter."

"Do you believe what you have been told, Wynter?" He slowly trailed his hand up her naked arm.

"I think I'd like to find out for myself." And with those words she raised herself onto her toes and pressed her lips against his, taking him by surprise. She brought her hands up to his chest and pushed against him, backing him into the alcove. Her lips never leaving his as she traced her tongue along his lips centre seam.

Florian allowed her to move him into the alcove, his arms moving to her waist, his mouth opening in response to her pressure and finding her questing tongue. While his mind raced to keep up with what was happening, his body responded on impulse. Carefully, as he didn't want to ruin her ball gown, he moved his hand up her rib cage and brushed the side of her breast. He pushed his hips against hers, showing her what she did to him.

Wynter broke off the kiss and looked up at him pressed against the wall. She took a tiny step back and fluttered her eyelashes at him before bringing her hand up between them and deliberately letting go of the flower he had given her moments before. "Oops," she whispered. "That was clumsy of me."

"Allow me to get that for you." He kissed her again. "I think we might have to swap places for me to get it though."

"If you think that best," she agreed before she pulled his head back down to her lips and they slowly turned until her back was against the wall.

Florian pulled away from her and in the shadows of the alcove could barely make out her face, but he understood clearly what she wanted when she reached up to his shoulders and pushed down. "The flower?" she reminded him.

"Anything you want, Wynter."

The prince knelt on the stone floor of the alcove and didn't even bother to find the dropped stem; instead, he picked her heavy skirts up and placed his hand on her slippered foot, and waited for a response. She simply moved her feet apart and waited. He grinned to himself as he slid his hand up her bare calf and got to her knee without any resistance or discovering clothing. His grin grew wider and his cock harder as he moved further under her skirts and let them drape over him, his fingers continuing to walk their way up her naked leg.

As he moved over her smooth thigh and came to her slick folds, he realized that this was a woman who had her own agenda and had calculated this with clear intent. He was shocked and turned on by this revelation. He didn't have time to wonder what her game was as he drew her leg over his shoulder and his thumb found her clit as her quiet moan silenced his thoughts and he took pleasure in giving her what she clearly wanted.

He licked and kissed her inner thigh as he continued to circle his thumb. She tasted of honey and milk, and he wanted to devour her. He raised his head and licked her opening, her thighs quivered slightly in response, and he kissed her there before he slid his tongue into her warmth. As he moved his tongue in and out, he put added pressure on her clit with his thumb, keeping up the circular pattern. She ground her hips and pushed into his face, another moan softly floating down to him. Not letting up with either his tongue or hand, he kept going until he felt her clench against him. Her breathing ragged and her body stilled before a final shiver made her knee bend and he caught her from slipping down the wall. He licked her from opening to clit, causing her to buck against him before he began to kiss her in intervals as he moved back down her naked leg, bringing the leg that had been over his shoulder back down to the floor.

He disentangled himself from her dress and resettled the hem around her feet, his hands moving around to find the discarded flower. Once he had found it he stood and held it out to Wynter. "Is that what you were after?"

She reached up and put her hands around his neck, drawing his mouth down to hers. Slowly, she moved him back around so he was now backed up against the alcove wall. As she pulled away she looked him squarely in the eye. Even in the shadows he could see the intensity in them. "It's a start," she almost purred.

He held still as her hands moved down to the top of his pants and she ran her finger around the inside of the band. Wynter stood on her tiptoes and kissed his lips softly as her hands rubbed over the front of his trousers, his hard cock throbbing to be set free. "Thank you," she whispered before she broke all contact and hurried up the dimly lit hallway to her waiting bodyguard.

Florian stood there for several seconds, trying to get his hard-on under control and his breathing back to normal. He began to chuckle to himself as he realized just what she had done. Bet or no bet, he would bed that woman if it was with his final breath. Another type of challenge had been issued, and again he would not back down.

2 DAYS

QUEEN WYNTER

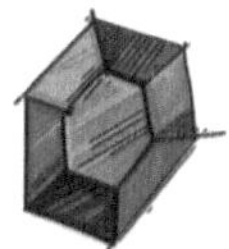

The grounds of the palace were perfectly maintained and Wynter took note of several ways they had partitioned off areas for certain activities without losing the feeling of sprawling space. Low hedges were common, rather than the high ones she had in her castle gardens. A thicket of small trees hid the side of the stables that would otherwise intrude on the vista that the higher placed palace had overlooking the sprawling rolling hills of the countryside and the sparkling sea to the left. Fountains and flower gardens dotted the area, all in geometric patterns, that she had admired from her suite window earlier that morning. Small stages with large canopies had been set up around the gardens where there were minstrels, bards, and dance troupes all performing different styles of entertainment to suit everyone's tastes. Someone had come up with the clever idea of setting up a large table that held baskets that contained food and drink. All you needed was to instruct the kitchen servant at the table how many you needed the basket for and you were handed a rug, basket, and a ceramic flagon of cider or mead that you could then take with you to whichever entertainer suited you. Folding chairs were available for the older nobles or the women who had chosen to wear dresses that were not suitable to easily get up and down from the ground.

Wynter had chosen to wear something in a light material and with only one underskirt as the weather was humid. Two of her handsome bodyguards walked behind her as she meandered by a pavilion that had a slightly larger stage that held a dance troupe of twelve girls in brightly colored costumes. She paused and watched, adding her applause when they had concluded their dance.

As Wynter turned to move away, she discovered Pierre walking toward her, and she put a smile on her face as he approached. He was a pleasant young man, but far too innocent for her liking. The heir to Viscount George's title bowed deeply before he spoke. "Your Majesty."

"Pierre." She nodded her head in greeting. "Did you enjoy yourself last night?"

"Very much so, and you?"

The unbidden memory of Florian's hands sliding up her bare leg made her smile warmly. "It was an enjoyable evening," she agreed.

"My uncle and I were wondering if you would like to join us for lunch?"

"Sorry, Pierre, but Her Majesty already promised me her company today," a voice spoke behind them.

They both turned to find Prince Florian standing next to Wynter's bodyguards, his own personal guard a step behind him, and Tumas standing to the side. Pierre bowed and Wynter smiled at the interloper. He was a stunning-looking man. His tanned skin glowed against his white linen shirt, opened at the front, showing his smooth chest. Wynter's stomach did a tiny flutter as she took in his hazel eyes, soft lips, and strong jawline. The prince made her insides clench as his look dared her to call him on the lie. "I was about to accept, and it would serve you right for making me wait, but I will honor my word." She smiled sweetly at him.

"I apologize for my tardiness, Your Majesty." He held out his crooked arm to her.

Wynter turned and placed her hand on the forearm of Pierre. "Please, thank your uncle for the offer. Perhaps I will see you both later." She let his arm go and looked to Florian, who she noted looked like he had swallowed something sour before his beautiful face cleared and a neutral expression was once again all he showed the world. Wynter took his proffered arm, and Tumas and their bodyguards fell in behind them.

"You will break his poor heart if you keep that up," Florian spoke mildly as he steered her toward the long trestle table filled with baskets, flagons, and folded rugs.

"Since when do you care about wounded suitors?"

Florian stayed silent as they walked and Wynter took the moment to enjoy the feeling of strolling around the gorgeous gardens and taking in all the entertainment. She smiled demurely at the eligible males they passed, all who nodded and watched her with the prince. It was a strategic move on her behalf to take his offered arm as it would clearly show that only those of high enough rank would be entertained as a companion to the queen. Poor Pierre and his Viscount title would never do, no matter how sweet he was.

"A basket and flagon of cider for two, please." Florian spoke to a young kitchen hand. He turned to her. "Is there anything you don't eat or don't like?"

Wynter shook her head. "No, anything is acceptable."

Tumas stepped forward and took the basket, flagon, and rug from the servant.

"Where would you like to eat? Is there any type of entertainment you prefer?" Florian asked as they turned away from the table.

"A quieter, less crowded place would be lovely. All these festivities are wearing a little thin for someone who not so long ago spent a lot of time alone in a forest," she confided in him.

"How about the edge of the trees over there? Away from the groups of people and in the shade, but you can still people watch and feel the atmosphere."

"Sounds perfect to me."

They followed the red cobblestone path, along a low-lying hedge toward the copse of small trees, with pretty yellow blossoms scattered on them. Wynter had her hand still looped over Florian's arm and she tried not to think about how natural it felt. The prince was a player and she found it attractive to turn the tables on him, but the trick would be not to fall for him while doing it.

"You are quiet today. Where is your usual charming banter? It's the only reason I said yes when you interrupted Pierre's invitation," she teased. She looked up and then quickly away as she saw a glint in his eyes; she did not want to be drawn into those hazel eyes.

"I was hoping for something more than playful banter today."

"Really?" For some reason that statement made her nervous.

They arrived near the trees and moved off the pathway and onto the lush green grass. Wynter and Florian both stood quietly as Tumas laid out the rug and placed the flagon and basket on the edge.

With reluctance, she let go of his arm, only to have him hold out his hand to help her sit on the rug. He truly was chivalrous in his manner. As Wynter tucked her legs under her pretty cotton yellow and white checked dress, she looked up at the smiling man. "If not banter, what were you hoping for?"

Florian sat down next to her, graceful as he moved his legs to one side and leaned to drag the basket closer to him.

Tumas stepped closer. "Allow me, Your Highness."

Florian waved away his servant. "I am perfectly capable of opening a basket and taking out food. Please go for a stroll, get some food, watch some dancing girls, but do not hover. I will take care of Her Majesty's needs."

Wynter hid her smile by looking down and picking a few small shafts of grass from her dress. She couldn't quite fathom why she found the exchange amusing, but she was happy to be sitting so close to the handsome man with no one but their bodyguards within hearing range. She flushed as her thoughts turned naughty and she shivered with ideas of all the different needs she had that he could fulfill if given enough time. Her cheeks warmed with the thought.

"Your Majesty, can I offer you a drink while I prepare our lunch?" He winked at her as Tumas walked away.

"That would be splendid, but again, please call me Wynter."

He inclined his head. "Very well."

Wynter watched him deftly remove two plain metal cups from the basket and held them out for her to take. He then took the flagon and worked the waxed cork out of the opening. He deftly poured them both a drink of the sparkling cider before re-stopping the flagon. She handed him a cup and he clinked his glass to hers before they both drank. Wynter closed her eyes as the surprisingly still cool liquid coated her parched throat.

"Will you tell me something private about yourself? There are so many rumors about you, and I would like to know something real," said Florian. His glorious eyes watched her with a steady gaze, and she almost flinched from the directness of it. This man brought out feelings in her she hadn't been aware existed and Wynter reminded herself to be careful. She had set out to play him at his own game, not get caught in it.

"Pick one rumor and I will tell you whether it is true or not, but—" She held up her hand to forestall a response. "I want something in return."

Florian raised an eyebrow and almost leered at her. She was sure the only thing that was keeping him from behaving was the many nobles strolling by. "Name your price," he said.

"Stop dawdling with the food, I am famished," she ordered.

"As you wish, Wynter." He bowed his shoulders and head.

Wynter watched the prince take out several wrapped

parcels and place them on a board that had covered the basket. He unwrapped a loaf of crusty bread, a wheel of soft cheese, a ceramic bowl of some type of brown spread, figs, grapes, and black currents. The final package held a type of cured, thinly sliced meat. There were several different knives in the bottom of the basket and two thick, red cloth napkins. Everything you could want for a perfect afternoon of relaxing with friends and loved ones while being entertained by the best the kingdom had to offer. Wynter watched with growing amusement as Florian set everything out on the board in a neat, cohesive fashion. By the time he was done, she was smiling broadly.

"What?" he asked as he finally moved his attention away from the board and food.

"Nothing." She decided not to make fun of him for this idiosyncrasy; she thought it was becoming. "Ask your question." Wynter tried to act nonchalant as she chose from the food platter he had created. She knew many rumors were doing the rounds about her, most had a grain of truth, but that was truly about all. It would be interesting to see what he wanted to know about her.

"This is so unfair," he groaned dramatically. "I want to know it all."

Wynter shrugged, but with a twinkle in her eye said, "We all have to deal with disappointment."

Florian laughed with a freedom he rarely showed and her heart jolted at the sound. He came across as casual and relaxed as if nothing could bother him. He was always carefree, cheerful, and charming, appearing to have it all together and not be bothered by the politics and pressures of being a part of the ruling noble family of the realm.

Wynter was hoping to see the underneath of it, to discover the real man and why he did what he did. His reputation was whispered about, and she wanted to know about the rest of him.

"Don't talk to me about disappointment." He continued to laugh. "I am not sure I forgive what you did last night."

Wynter knew this conversation could quickly spiral into flirting and superficial chit-chat—she didn't want that. She was interested in what he wanted to know about her. The queen took a red grape and popped it in her mouth, giving herself a moment to figure out how to draw him back to the conversation that would hopefully reveal more of him and give her the chance to reveal more of herself. She had no idea why this was important to her. Things were becoming more complicated than she had anticipated when she had decided to engage with his flirting that first night at the feast. Wynter decided that the direct approach could possibly work the best on Florian, he probably was used to women being coy and demure, and the up-front angle the other night had worked like a charm and left him longing for more. Whether she decided to give it to him was yet to be determined. "Your question?"

"Why are you not with your predestined prince?"

The Queen of the Fourth Kingdom was a tad taken aback by the question. She had been expecting a different response.

Wynter held up her cup, waiting for a refill. She arched an eyebrow at him but didn't speak for several moments as she pondered what to tell him. "I don't want to be told what to do by anyone. My life has been reacting to things happening to me rather than being in control of situations.

That a single kiss could seal my fate, without me having a say, just infuriated me. Who gets to decide that?" She stopped and took a sip of her cider for a moment, gathering her thoughts. "I do look at Ashe and Dawn, who both chose to accept their path, and they appear happy, but are they?"

For a moment, a look crossed Florian's handsome face that she wasn't used to. Doubt. Wynter shook off the odd look and went on. "I want to make my own choices. Whether they are disastrous or my greatest victories, I want them to be mine." Wynter stopped and hoped she had not revealed too much of herself.

Florian smiled and reached for the flagon. After taking the stopper out, he wrapped his hand around her smaller one that held the cup as if to steady it. "I want to kiss you again," he murmured as the liquid-filled the plain cup.

A slow fire began to creep from the center of her core, fanning the flames that had been simmering since last night. There was so much at stake, and she wanted to do this right. A clearing of the throat interrupted her next words.

Florian let go of her hand and they both turned to face the interloper. The young, thin blond man with his pinched features bowed deeply to both of them. Wynter smiled politely. "Please excuse the intrusion. I thought it the perfect time to come and allow Prince Florian to introduce me to his guest."

The prince stood slowly, obviously annoyed at the intrusion. Florian held out his hand and helped her stand. The interloper averted his eyes in deference to the monarch. The queen waited for Florian to do the introductions, pretending to not know the man standing before them, and hiding her dismay as he had interrupted what could have been a wonderful moment. Now she would have to find another time to continue their cat and mouse game. The Queen of the Fourth Kingdom turned her full attention to the man before them as she knew his secret and couldn't afford for him to detect any lies as she followed through on the main reason she had accepted the invitation to the week-long ceremony.

Florian

Florian smiled benignly and managed to stop himself from openly groaning when Stic interrupted what was becoming a fascinating conversation. He had been about to bring everything back around to ask the question concerning if she had a treasured thing from those times living in the woods. He figured it would reveal something or lead him into discovering what her most valued possession was. The question about her walking away from her supposed fated mate was just something he had wanted to know. He found it fascinating that his sisters-in-law just accepted that the men who had saved them were their true loves without any hesitation. It was almost absurd when you took the time to think about it.

The queen was wonderful to be around, but he also knew she had an agenda; why else would she come? She had too much going on in her own country to take time to travel to the Kingdom of Dreams for an engagement party without an ulterior motive. The more he thought about it, the more he wanted to know what Wynter was truly doing here. What had begun as a simple seduction and then turned into a challenge had now grown into a tantalizing conundrum that he wanted to unravel.

He grasped her hand firmly as he helped her rise to greet the interloper. The current that ran through her hand and straight to his groin was difficult to ignore. Florian wanted to make an excuse to get her to leave with him so he could take her to his rooms and take her over and over. He needed to possess this woman in a way that terrified yet thrilled him.

"Please allow me to introduce my friend, Baron Rupert Stictson." He made the introduction formally, and just happened to be watching Wynter's face as she looked at Stic. The queen seemed cautious, almost hesitant, to meet Stic. Florian looked to Stic who appeared to be completely oblivious to the look on Wynter's face, and was openly ogling the young queen—maybe it wasn't only men he liked. It was not a discussion the friends had openly had, as it didn't bother Florian either way—until Stic had tried to kiss him.

"Your Majesty." The Baron bowed.

"Baron." Wynter spoke in that cool tone she had used with Florian on the first night they had spoken at the feast, but it was only now that he recognized she had stopped sounding glacial toward him. Her tone was inviting, warm, and filled with humor when they were alone.

As Stic engaged Queen Wynter in small talk, Florian noted Tumas striding purposely toward them. Behind him, it looked like several other nobles were walking in their direction. Tumas bowed curtly to Florian and spoke in a low voice. "It would appear the dour faces of your combined bodyguards is no longer enough to keep everyone at bay now that the Baron has joined you."

"Yes, it seems that way. Would you please pack up the food and cloth; I don't think we will require it any longer."

"Of course, Your Highness."

Florian smiled warmly at the first nobles to arrive. "Welcome. Your timing is impeccable. I have monopolized enough of the queen's time, and before I outstay my welcome, was about to take my leave." He winked at the sisters, who were both wed to old doddery men, and he had taken advantage of that boredom several times. They twittered their amusement before turning to be introduced to the queen.

Several more of the younger nobles, or their offspring, were drawn to the small group standing under the shade of the pretty trees, and soon there were about ten of them with Wynter standing in the middle, her slightly crisp accent making her mysterious and a novelty. Florian bowed and murmured that he was off to find liquor, chairs, and servants to carry them to the impromptu gathering. No one considered that he could have simply sent Tumas, as he would have enough clout to order other servants to do his bidding. Wynter smiled but did not say anything as he moved away, and Florian had to admit he was mildly disappointed that she didn't seem to mind if he stayed or not.

The sun was bright after being in the shade for so long and he blinked several times as he and Tumas walked across the grass and back to the path that led through the gardens. Florian was silent and trying not to dwell on the incredible

Wynter when he came to the large, high hedge that was a corner to the perfectly manicured maze that took up a large portion of his mother's favorite part of the garden. He walked the path, watching people exit and enter the maze with varying degrees of trepidation and relief. The maze was not simple to navigate, but he had mastered it as a child as he and his brothers were timed at how quickly they could find their way through, as a means to train their memories.

A large group of people sat or stood around the opening, probably waiting for the more adventerous ones of their friends and family who had chosen to try their hand at the queen's maze. Suddenly, the crowd parted and Florian spotted Ashe, who smiled and waved and appeared to look determined to make her way to him. Not wanting to extricate himself out of a situation he had created, he chose to duck into the entrance of the maze rather than face the determined-looking princess.

Inside the entrance, he stopped and turned to Tumas. "Go and get the chairs and liquor organized for Queen Wynter and the group that is with her. I want to see if I can still traverse the maze without a wrong turn," he lied. "Wish me luck."

"Good luck, Your Highness." Tumas bowed and left via the entrance.

Florian made his way deeper into the maze with his bodyguard trailing behind him. He was surprised at how quickly he recalled which turns to take. Several people stopped to engage him in conversation, but as he meandered through, the crowd thinned out as they got lost and turned around. The prince attempted to put the gnawing feeling that he was running out of time out of his head as he calculated that he only had two days left to sleep with Wynter and Dawn, as well as learn their most prized possessions and then figure out how to take them without getting caught with all the extra guards roaming the palace at the moment. He was still not ready to admit he had perhaps taken on a challenge he could not meet. The idea was unthinkable for several reasons; he had to win and that meant staying calm and finding a way.

As he was walking through the maze without taking much notice of his surroundings, it was no surprise when he turned a corner and almost walked into a woman standing still. This was the center of the maze and there were several options to take. "You want that one," he said quietly into the ear of the woman.

The Queen of the Moors gave a small yelp and her bodyguard spun to find out why. Florian took a step back and held up his hands and the brute of a man glowered at him. "You scared me," she said unnecessarily.

"Can you forgive me?" He widened his eyes and feigned innocence.

"If you get me out of this maze I will forgive you and owe you my gratitude."

"If I get you out of this maze without making one wrong turn, I think we can come up with a more suitable gift than just your gratitude."

Cornflower blue eyes gazed at him and he noted her tongue slide across her bottom lip before she caught it between her teeth. "Lead the way," Dawn finally spoke and gestured in front of her. Her guard stepping aside, allowing him to escort her forward.

He couldn't believe how quickly his luck had turned

from being interrupted by Stic when he had been steering Wynter in the direction of revealing what he needed to know, to running into Queen Dawn, lost and alone, and he now had the chance to perhaps steer their conversation in the right direction. Florian held out his arm to Dawn, just as he had done to Wynter earlier that day, and just like the dark-haired queen before her, this fair-haired one politely took his arm and they began to walk.

"I was having the most interesting conversation with Princess Ashe the other day about sentimental items and prized possessions," Florian said.

The bathwater was bitingly hot as he sunk into the large tub. A satisfied sigh escaped Florian's lips as he leaned back and the water rose to cover his shoulders. He was one step closer to his goal and the moments of self-doubt he had felt earlier that day had dissipated and been replaced by his more normal self-belief. He would win this bet and claim his prize. And he would feel no guilt for what he did. He wasn't coercing the women, they all had free will; he wasn't cheating on anyone, he was breaking no vows. He conveniently pushed aside the ramifications that if caught, his dalliances could create chaos for the relation-ships between Wynter's Kingdom, Dawn's, and his own country. He thrived on the adrenaline of the situation; he found it intoxicating.

Dawn's crown and Ashe's slippers. Two out of three objects were now known thanks to his little side trip into the maze today to avoid Ashe, and it had turned out quite fortuitously when he had discovered a lost and alone Dawn. It had surprised him when the beautiful, blonde queen confessed that her solid gold crown was the thing she cherished the most, but once she had explained, it had made perfect sense; after all, she had hinted at it as they danced at last night's ball. Dawn's crown represented all she had lost when she had succumbed to the curse of the wicked fairy and had slept for a century while her kingdom and family mourned and died. Yet, the crown to her also represented her future as a queen and that she could rebuild her life and country and gain all that she had lost. Dawn had said the words with sadness and steel and Florian had said all the right things while he secretly rejoiced at learning this new piece of information.

Her blue eyes had glittered with unshed tears by the end of the conversation, and rather than turn it to suggestions of comforting her in other ways, Florian had chosen to show his softer side and simply embrace her chastely and tell her how sorry he was that this had all happened to her.

"Your Highness." Tumas interrupted Florian's pleasant thoughts by tapping politely on the door of the bathing room. "I have laid your clothes out for tonight's festivities. Is there anything else you require?"

"No, thank you. Take an early supper as I will need you at my side tonight to run interference for me. I get the feeling the Baron Stictson is attempting to foil my plans." Florian frowned as he thought about Stic interrupting his lunch with Wynter earlier.

"Very well, I shall return within a candlemark."

Florian picked up the scented soap and lathered his

arms, his mind wandering as he washed himself. "I am going to need a plan," he said to himself before dipping his head under the water to rinse the soap from his close-cropped dark hair. *I am going to have to steal them all at once, as once it is discovered one is missing the palace will be on high alert and all the nobles and their guards will be wary, making it harder to get in to take the rest. But what order would be best?* he asked himself.

Would it be best to take Dawn and Wynter's possessions first as they were the furthest from his suite—people would be more likely to notice him in those corridors—and then head to the family wing where he could roam freely? That way if it was uncovered that the items were taken before he had the last one he would still have a better chance of getting to it as he lived in the right section and no one would think it odd when he walked around the royal wing? The idea had merit. Though, on the other hand, if he did the royal wing first and if they found one thing missing they would hopefully concentrate on that area and try to keep it quiet, thus allowing him to take Dawn and Wynter's possession without too much fuss. This plan also had its pros and cons.

And he would need a distraction so most people were not in their rooms. There was precious little time left to choose from. Tonight was the theatre, tomorrow afternoon the betrothal ceremony, and that would be followed by an evening of speeches, feasting, and dancing as the week of festivities finally concluded, with everyone planning on leaving and returning to their estates the following day.

You don't have to make any final decisions yet, he reminded himself. *You still have to seduce two of them.*

Florian grew hard at the idea of bedding Wynter. The thought was tantalizing and he considered taking care of himself, and though the thought was tempting, he refrained. A picture of Dawn's oval face filled his mind, her eyes closed and her blonde hair surrounded her as she slept. He had thought about kissing her awake for so long, but once Wynter had arrived, his desires and dreams about Dawn had been replaced with the picture of a rounder face, with a cute button nose and darker eyes and hair. The shy, demure personality that was Dawn was sweet and perfect for his brother; he could see that now. He desired someone who could match him and challenge him, and until this moment, he had not known that that was something he wanted. Wynter, with her cool exterior, strong self-dependence, and wanton behavior in the corridor the evening of the ball made him think about her more than any other woman he had ever known. It was disquieting and he didn't know what to make of it.

Water sloshed out of the tub as Florian stood abruptly. Trying to ignore his hard-on and growing desires, he refocused on what he needed to do to win this bet. *I hope once I bed her she will become to me just like the rest—another pleasant memory.* He grabbed the towel that hung from a hook and put it over his head, rubbing it vigorously to dry his hair.

"Well, well, well," a female voice whistled softly.

He smiled behind the towel.

*P*rince Florian brought the towel down slowly, and he smiled at what he found standing in the doorway to his bathing room. Queen Wynter stood there, her shapely legs and arms bare, the only thing covering her feminine assets was his olive green vest, which she held closed with clenched fists. His wide grin when he heard her greeting now turned to a slow sensuous smile. With calculated ease, Florian didn't bother to hide himself with his towel, he simply let it slide from his hand and pool at his wet feet. He worked hard for his toned body and was happy to flaunt it. "Can I help you with something?" he asked.

Her brilliant brown eyes started at his feet and traveled up his body, a predatory stare clear on her face. Florian's lower abs fluttered and clenched as he swelled further. This woman was incredible, and though he had a suspicion that she played her own game, at this moment, it didn't matter; all his brain and cock could recognize was that she was voluntarily standing almost naked before him. "I thought I would see if you were interested in finishing what we started the other night?" she almost purred.

He licked his lips but didn't move. "I am sure I could be persuaded."

Wynter arched a dark eyebrow at him and let her hands fall to reveal that she was indeed naked under his vest. The swell of her breasts was visible, and a dark triangle of hair was exposed at the apex of her legs. He swallowed and lifted his hand and crooked his index finger at her, beckoning Wynter to come closer. With a giggle that didn't match the cool queen's persona, but perfectly fit the young woman, she made her way over to him. Without a word, she dropped to her knees before him, resting on the abandoned towel rather than the cold, hard flagstone of the bathing room. The dark-haired beauty looked up at him through her thick lashes for several moments before she reached up with her small hand and took hold of his cock, running her thumb along the seam and over the rim.

His body responded and he moaned with pleasure as he planted his feet wider and firmer on the ground. Wynter took him into her mouth and Florian's core flamed in response. The way her tongue swirled around his head and the sucking pressure she used made him push his hips forward. The sensation was mind-blowing, and he panted as his climax grew. She moved her hand up and down, holding him tight at the base as she sucked hard on the head, and he thought his knees might collapse under him as he fought to walk the fine line of continued pleasure and release. Wynter's other hand snaked its way over his lower abs and came to rest under his rib cage. She slowly drew her hand back down, applying enough pressure that her nails dug into his skin and left a red trail on his flesh along with a wonderful stinging sensation.

Before he could explode in her mouth, he bent slightly and put his hands under her arms and pulled her up. As he lifted her, he didn't stop when she was upright; instead, he changed the position of his hands under her arms and with little effort continued to lift her until her face was level with his. Wynter wrapped her legs around his waist, and he felt the wetness of her folds against him. Florian carried her, moving one hand to her soft ass and the other around her back.

They shared an intense stare as he pushed her up

against the wall. "You are beautiful," he told her, hoping she realized he meant it.

She smiled shyly at him. "Kiss me."

Florian leaned in and pressed his parted lips to hers; their passion flared and his cock twitched at her entrance. As he deepened the kiss, a tiny moan escaped her and his mind went wild. Her arm wrapped around his neck and her hand moved to the back of his head, holding him so she could press her lips firmer to his, her talented tongue demanding attention. Wynter moved her hips and Florian found himself inside her by a fraction, and he pushed his hips forward and slid deeper still. The warmth, wetness, and tightness of her were incredible, and his cock and core responded. Slowly, he pulled out and slid back in, each time going a little further, pacing himself and building the sensations between them. Her hands held onto his shoulders and her feet pushed into his ass, telling him exactly what she wanted.

The bathing room was filled with panting and grunts as Florian threw away all his courtly breeding and thrust into Wynter hard and fast, over and over. The queen bent her head and bit his shoulder, causing him to yell in surprise rather than pain. The sensation was shocking, but also welcome. She dragged her nails down his back as he pounded into her, pinning her to the wall. His orgasm built until he could hold it no longer, and with a final deep thrust, he pumped his seed inside her, only dimly aware of her stilling before she groaned and her muscles clamped around him, making him shudder as she drew out the final intense moments of his climax with her own.

Florian kissed her sweetly, a tender one on her lips, then one on the tip of her cute nose. "You got time for a bath?"

"I thought you would want to hustle me out of here." She winked at him as she ran her thumb over his bottom lip.

"Not you. Never." He kissed her again and lifted her gently off him and set her on her feet. "May I take your vest, Your Majesty?"

Wynter turned to allow him to slowly pull the satin fabric off her shoulders. He noted the back of it was ruined from being rubbed against the stone wall—better the vest than her back, he figured. Florian tossed it aside and bent to kiss her neck. "Unless you want to run away now you have had your way with me," he murmured against her snow-white skin.

Rather than the giggle like before he was met with a throaty laugh. "Oh, I am not done with you yet." And with those words, Florian allowed himself to be led back to his tub.

As he slid down into the now warm water, he was grateful it had cooled as the scratches that now adorned his body only stung a little before the heat soothed them. He watched Wynter as she settled on the other side of the tub and smiled knowingly at him. He wondered how he was going to work the subject around to her favorite thing and get her to agree to another tryst all within the next candlemark.

Who are you kidding? he asked himself as he closed his eyes and enjoyed the moment. *This is your skill set, you have got more than one woman to tell you more intimate things than this. You are not known as Prince Charming for no reason. Now put your charms to work.*

Florian opened his eyes to discover Wynter had floated closer while he had closed his eyes. There was a gleam in her eyes that made him grab her and haul her onto his lap, and she did not resist. "What are you thinking about?"

He almost laughed as the most uttered phrase by women fell out of her mouth. It was totally unexpected, but gave him the opening he was looking for.

The bodyguard's face was impassive as Florian, wrapped only in a towel, opened his door to allow Wynter to leave. He patted her perfect bottom as she walked out, and winked after she turned to glare at him. Before Wynter could come up with some witty comment, Florian closed the door. He smiled broadly to himself as he imagined what her expression may be at his actions before spinning and heading back into his bedroom and opening the large closet to find a new vest to wear for the evening's festivities, as the one Tumas had laid out was completely ruined. He quickly selected one similar to the one that had been laid out for him, and then headed to the bathing room.

In his typical fashion, Florian had left the bathroom in disarray; he had refilled the tub for them both to wash in after their second love-making session and it was still draining. Towels lay strewn on the floor and the discarded vest that Wynter had worn was soggily sitting in a corner. Florian picked his way through the debris, sponges, lotions, and unguents had been knocked over from their shelf beside the tub. It truly looked like a whirlwind had landed in the center of the room. He picked up a comb and carried it out of the room to the sound of the final dregs of water gurgling down the center plug hole.

Moving back into the bedroom, he came to stand before the full-length mirror to run a comb through his hair. Though it was short, it still tended to dry flat in places if he didn't comb it. He smiled to himself as he noted the scratch marks on his shoulders and twisted to see if there were any on his back. There were several long red welts and his stomach fluttered at the sight and the memory of how they got there and by whom. It would be a pleasant reminder until they healed.

Florian whistled happily as he began to dress for the evening's festivities. A night at the theater seemed far less stressful now that he had ticked two more of the challenges that had been issued. Ashe had been the easiest to seduce and divulge that the stunning diamond slippers that had led to her being found were her most prized possession. Wynter now joined that list. While she had made the challenge of seduction far more entertaining, in the end, she had succumbed to his charms. Wynter had divulged that her prized possession was a ruby in the shape of an apple that was what her stepmother had used to try to kill her. It showed she was a survivor.

Dawn was still his biggest challenge. Florian didn't know what was going to be more difficult: getting Dawn to say yes or not getting caught stealing everything. He wondered if he would have the opportunity to speak to her alone tonight. Maybe flirt subtly. He thought about the differences in the three women he had been pursuing and how he had had to change his behavior to suit their personalities. Wynter was bold and after a shaky start, he had quickly learned that the game was as fun for her as it was for him. Ashe had been far easier to seduce than he had anticipated and until now he was just grateful and hadn't thought about it, but as he adjusted his tie, he wondered if there had been a reason for her to betray his brother as soon as Florian had commenced his campaign. Warning bells went off. The thought was unsettling, but he didn't have time to consider it further—nor did his nature truly want him to—as then he would need to truly acknowledge what he had done to one brother and was hoping to do to another. Given they were both arrogant prigs who had lorded it over him as a child, he felt justified in his actions as only the self-righteous do. He knew himself well enough to acknowledge it and not care.

Florian looked at the timekeeper on the mantle above the fireplace as he walked into his private sitting room. He had just enough time to have a shot of his favorite liquor before he had to meet his family and join the ride to the royal theater. As he walked to the liquor trolley there was a sharp rap on the door before it was opened by one of his guards and Tumas walked in, followed by Stic.

"Pour me one, would you?" his friend asked as his servant raised an eyebrow but said nothing at the way Stic spoke to the prince in other's company.

Florian's servant was a master at conveying almost anything with just the movement of his eyebrows. The prince noted both brows furrow slightly as Tumas took in the different vest to the one that had been laid out. He winked in response and was rewarded with rolled eyes. To stop himself from chuckling and having to answer to Stic as to why he was suddenly laughing, he busied himself making the second drink.

The friends clinked their brilliant crystal-cut glasses together and Florian settled down into a low armchair under a window that spilled in the last of the late afternoon's light. They often sat in the two well-worn chairs and passed the time with idle chatter and playing chess. But there had been no games and little inconsequential chit-chat for many months now. Florian had grown uncomfortable spending candlemarks with his friend alone as he had to keep his guard up once it had been clear that Stic could always see the truth when he or someone asked a question. That was the reason that Florian had finally accepted this bet, as it was the only way to uncover the truth. It was a complicated gamble and he had had to bide his time and not look too eager or Stic would have gotten suspicious. When the issue had been challenged to bed his sisters-in-law, Florian had not cared at all who he hurt, and he still didn't. He liked women and they liked him, and he would use that to his advantage until he didn't need to anymore. Though, Wynter was becoming a different thing. She came up in his thoughts far more than any woman ever had, and he hoped now that he had bedded her she would return to being just another conquest.

The baron moved around the room until he came to stand beside a small cage, no larger than the size of his hand, that stood on a round marble table in the far corner, tucked away so no one would notice it unless they moved to that area. Stic bent down and looked in the gold cage. Florian watched but said nothing. The occupant of that cage was a secret that only Florian, Stic, and Tumas knew about and it was never discussed. "Any trouble?" Stic asked.

"No, the cage seems to keep her under control, like promised." Florian took another sip of his drink.

Stic moved away from the corner and stood before the empty fireplace. "So, tell me, how is the bet proceeding?" Stic asked.

Florian chose his words carefully; he didn't want to reveal how many things he had accomplished in the three-fold challenge. "Surprising. Though, I could have throttled you this morning when you interrupted my private lunch with Queen Wynter. I was about to engage her in conversation regarding her prized possession when you rudely intruded upon our meal." None of what Florian said was untrue, and he was pleased with his cleverness.

"Your Majesty, it is time to leave." Tumas entered the room carrying a cloak.

"I think it might be a little warm for that," Florian said, eyeing the cloak.

"This is for the return home. I will bring it with me."

"Very well." Florian drained his glass and put it on a nearby table as he stood and stretched. He looked to his friend. "Shall we?" Stic looked as if he wanted to protest, but his prince had risen and invited him to leave, there was little he could do but follow or cause offense and he had already pushed his friendship twice for the day.

1 DAY

FLORIAN

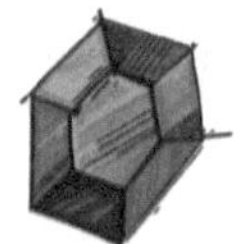

The shiny azure blue ribbon was spooled in the open palm of his hand as he contemplated his next move. Florian had spent an unproductive and somewhat frustrating night at the theater. He had been diverted, interrupted, and detained whenever he had attempted to get close to Dawn, while he also continued to avoid Ashe, and watched with growing unease as Wynter flirted with several men; one, a prince from a far off kingdom where his dark skin and colorful long robes were the norms. His thoughts dwelled on her pretty, smiling face and her hand resting on the exotic prince's arm, and Florian's insides bunched up in a way he couldn't understand. *Figure it out another time, you still have a queen to bed, and she gets betrothed to your brother after lunch.*

Closing his fist over the ribbon, Florian decided to visit Queen Dawn now. The family would have finished breaking their fast and would be deep in preparation for the day's special ceremony. She should be in her private rooms, which were near Queen Wynter's in the guest wing of the palace. Until the queen and Prince Phillip were wed, they kept separate rooms; though, they did spend many hours together, Florian knew not a lot of it was alone, as it would appear unseemly.

His personal bodyguards made to walk behind him when he halted and spoke under his breath so only they could hear. "I will be using the servants' tunnels and won't be leaving the palace grounds. You know what to do." Both the men looked at him and nodded before falling back into standing on either side of his door, as if guarding the occupant inside. The older of the two, who had been his personal guard for a few years, gave him a sly wink before returning to his duties. If questioned, they would tell callers that the prince was indisposed and not able to receive visitors at the moment. If people became insistent then they would call upon Tumas to deal with the situation, but no one ever gave away that the prince was not in his quarters.

Florian hurried down the wide hall until he found a wood panel slightly darker than the rest. It was nestled in between two paintings of cherubs that his mother had commissioned years prior. The service door for the servants to come and go in the family wing slid open as he pushed on the top right corner, startling a maid with an armload of clean sheets. Florian stepped aside and let her into the hallway before ducking into the small space. He placed a finger to his lips, and the maid smiled slightly; like the other servants, they had been witness to Florian's antics for so long that no one thought much of it when he used the tunnels. They all knew he was using them to visit someone he shouldn't, and as no one wanted to lose their job by tattling on the prince, everyone kept silent. *Who was he hurting?* tended to be the consensus.

The maid closed the panel and Florian stopped for a moment to allow his eyes to adjust to the dim lighting of the narrow tunnels. It was like a rabbit warren within the walls of the palace, and one could easily get lost, as he had done when he first decided to explore them while hiding from his governess many years ago. There were large torches in blackened sconces unevenly spaced out, casting shadows and dim light to see by. Florian set off in the direction of the guest's wing.

As he walked, he encountered several palace servants all carrying out their daily tasks, while several more, who looked to be a little frazzled, he guessed were charged with important things to do with the afternoon's betrothal ceremony. He stepped aside for all of them, rather than the other way around, as he was essentially intruding upon their space. They either nodded or murmured polite greetings in passing, but no one was surprised to see him.

Eventually, he reached the closest hidden door to Dawn's suite's and slowly slid the panel open. He waited for a moment, trying to hear if there was anyone in the corridor. It appeared empty. He inched his head forward and looked both ways before quickly stepping out and closing the panel. Florian hurried down the elaborately decorated hallway until he reached Queen Dawn's rooms. Her bodyguards in their red and black armor looked imposing, but neither stopped him as he raised his hand to knock on her door. He noted that both men, though powerfully built, were not as handsome as Wynter's impressive seven.

The knock was answered promptly by a plain-faced

young woman, who curtsied deeply and moved aside for him to enter without asking a single question. She closed the door behind him and indicated for him to sit before disappearing into another room.

"Your Highness?" an older woman walked briskly into the room, curtsied, and waited for him to state his business with the queen.

"I would like to speak privately with Queen Dawn for a few moments. I am aware she has a full schedule today." He was arrogant, his posture relaxed. "While I wait, a cup of meadow's tea would be appreciated."

The older woman nodded in response and exited through the same door the plain-faced girl had gone. Florian could just make out a hushed conversation before the door was again opened and out stepped the beautiful Queen of the Moors. She wore a pale pink robe, cinched at the waist and matching slippers. Her wealth of blond hair, which he found so appealing, was held back with a kerchief, showing her flawless dewy skin. Florian stood and bowed, though his eyes never left hers. "Your Majesty, you look radiant on this auspicious day."

She flushed. "Thank you, Prince Florian."

He wasted no time in getting to the point; he felt the moments ticking by and his chance slipping out of his grasp. He held out his hand and opened his fingers, revealing the ribbon he had purchased earlier in the week. "I saw it and thought of you. In the years to come, when you look back at this time and this gift, I hope you remember me fondly."

Queen Dawn

*D*awn looked at the ribbon in the charming prince's hand, offered as a gesture, but the accepting would mean more and they both knew it. Florian had made it clear that he desired her, that he wished for things to be different, and while the thought was appealing she knew she was marrying the right man.

Phillip was honorable, kind, brave, and she owed him a great deal of gratitude for slaying the witch who had transformed herself into a dragon and freeing Dawn from the century-old curse. Phillip had become the family she had lost, and she loved him. But a voice whispered to her in the night now Florian had suggested it, and she had met Wynter, who had gone against the preordained structures of curses, and Dawn couldn't help but wonder if she was missing out on something. She would remain faithful for the remainder of her life once she was officially betrothed, but she was young and that at the moment, felt like the rest of her life was an eternity.

Florian was as desirable as his brother and had many of his own qualities. He was funny, kind, and thoughtful. Dawn knew after seeing him win the archery contest that he was more than capable of defending himself and those he cared for, and would probably have succeeded in slaying the dragon as efficiently as his brother had. The last two nights she had dreamt of those moments when she had awakened from her enforced slumber, and it was Florian's face hovering over hers. He was also a womanizer, bedding anyone he chose; though, he was always discreet and never spoke about his conquests, others did. Usually, the woman herself was quick to discuss it with her friends and that is when the rumors started. She was certain that if she chose that path, he would never divulge the secret that they would share, and at the end that was the deciding factor. He was trustworthy in keeping the secret.

Queen Dawn wanted the happy ever after the lifting of the curse promised her, but she wanted it, like Queen Wynter, on her own terms. And with the decision made, she reached out and covered his open hand with her own.

His eyes widened for a moment, but he covered it with a shy smile." You will accept my gift?"

"Yes." Dawn took the ribbon, and she ran it through her fingers, enjoying the feel of the silky satin. "I want your help with something."

"Anything."

"I have had several conversations with Queen Wynter and will admit to being fascinated by the sheer audacity she has displayed by throwing aside the constraints of her destiny and following her own path." Dawn paused and gave him a small smile. "I do not wish to do anything that dramatic, but I would like to at least confirm that Phillip is the one fated for me, and it wasn't chance that he, and not you, kissed me."

Florian tilted his head to the side and studied her. "Are you sure this is what you want?"

"Yes," Dawn said firmly, certain of her decision.

"How do you plan on realizing if you truly love Phillip or if it could have been me?"

"You are going to get your wish."

Florian frowned.

"My young maid will be out in a few moments to prepare your meadow tea; a servant should be here any moment with it. Take your time and enjoy it. Once my lady-in-waiting also joins you, slowly count to one hundred and then you may enter." Dawn gestured toward the door.

Comprehension showed on his face and she watched him lick his lips with anticipation, something within her twisted, it was unexpected and wonderful. "Thank you for the gift." She held up the ribbon and nodded her head before she stepped through the door and into her luxurious bedchamber.

Her lady-in-waiting hovered nearby, pretending to work on her needlepoint when in reality she wanted to know what her queen was up to. Maggie, the young maid, had finished making the bed and was straightening the few personal items that sat on Dawn's bedside table. "Maggie, the tea for the prince should be here any moment, please wait in the other room and make him what he requires." The plain-faced girl nodded her head and went to leave. "And, please remember discretion is important. Take the tray from the servant at the door; we do not need my reputation tarnished by a gossiping palace servant."

Maggie gave a quick curtsy in agreeance and left the room. Dawn turned to the Lady Hammond, a far-off relative who had become a treasured friend and confidant. "I have decided to make sure I was kissed by the correct prince and have a little fun in the process." Dawn's eyes sparkled as she revealed her true nature. Yes, she was quiet and reserved, but in private she was playful and daring. You just needed to be trusted by her and a part of her inner sanctum, not many people were lucky to pass the test.

Lady Hammond put aside the needlework and grinned. "He is devilishly handsome."

"Fetch my blue gown, we must not tarry. I do not have much time before my vows and my fate is sealed."

Dawn untied the scarf from her head, allowing her soft curls to frame her face. Picking up a bottle of perfume, she dabbed it on her throat and wrists. Her stomach did another flip flop at the thought of Florian pressing himself against her like he did when they had danced, and she was surprised that it was as strong in sensation as when she thought about Phillip.

"Here is your gown," Lady Hammond announced as she walked into the room from a small dressing area that her clothing had been stored in.

Neither woman spoke as Dawn took off her soft pink dressing gown, revealing her lace hemmed drawers and bodice, and put on the azure blue gown that she had been found in, suspended in time, and waiting for her rescuer. Lady Hammond helped with the few buttons, and then after giving the queen a quick wink she left the room.

Once the door was closed, Dawn picked up her heavy gold crown and moved it to her bedside table. She sat on the edge of her bed for a few moments, waiting to see if guilt rose to the surface, and was greeted with excitement and a naughty thrill. She swung her legs around and rearranged her skirts before picking up the crown and holding it on her head as she lay back on the pillow. Adjusting it so it sat right, she smiled to herself as she thought of what was to come. Dawn brought her hands down to rest on her midsection and closed her eyes and waited. The anticipation fanned her flame of longing.

Florian

Her thick, halo of golden hair lay fanned out on her pillow, leaving her face and neck exposed. Her hands were folded, one on top of the other, resting upon her lower stomach. Her azure blue dress with its sweetheart neckline, tight long sleeves, fitted bodice, and the flowing skirt was exactly how he remembered it when he had watched over her while his brother had gone to battle the dragon. She had been a true sleeping beauty and he could have stood there and watched the steady rise and fall of her chest as she slumbered for days on end, but all too soon, his brother had returned the conquering hero and claimed a kiss from the princess who was truly a queen.

Florian stood there a moment longer, slowly turning the lock, savoring the sight, and willing her not to change her mind before he could taste her. With great care, he walked across the room and sat beside her, the mattress sagging sightly with his weight and making her roll a fraction toward him. Dawn continued to feign sleep, and he gave an inward sigh that she wanted to continue to play his suggested game. Florian put his hands on either side of her, not touching her, and leaned over to kiss her. He stopped a fraction from her perfectly shaped face and took in the smooth cheeks, high forehead, straight nose, and pointed chin. She smelled of grass and outdoors with an exotic undertone that most assuredly came from the time she spent with the others in the non-human realm of her country. For a split second, he almost called the whole thing off, his conscious getting the better of him, but then her chest rose with a deep breath and it drew his attention to her full breasts and his cock twitched, fueling his desire and crushing any thought of doing the right thing. Florian bent to kiss her.

Dawn's lips were soft and sweet. He felt her slightly give under the gentle pressure he applied, and her full lips opened a fraction, allowing him to run his tongue along the seam. He kissed her again, darting his tongue in and seeking hers. Florian slowly drew her tongue out and they twined together. Dawn quietly moaned and he suppressed the urge to whoop at the sound.

Florian didn't break contact, he assumed that if she had a chance to think, she would halt what he was about to do. He had to keep her off balance and lost in the sensations and heat of the encounter. He didn't speak, thinking that while she kept her eyes closed she could go on pretending it was her soon-to-be husband kissing her, and Florian's voice would break that illusion.

He moved one hand, slowly tracing his finger along the neckline of her dress, and he felt her skin respond with a shiver to his touch. Dawn reached up and she lifted her head slightly so she could remove the crown. Florian broke the kiss and covered her hands with his, taking the crown from her. He noted how heavy it was as he placed it gently on the bedside table.

He hovered over her, watching and waiting for what she would do next. The kiss had been sealed, the moment taken. Dawn lay back down, her cornflower blue eyes dark with desire. She bit her bottom lip and smiled. Florian didn't need any further invitation. He lowered his head and kissed her with passion. His cock hard, his core burning. The build-up of the delicate dance he had been forced to perform had made the anticipation of this moment almost unbearable. "Florian," she breathed against his lips.

That one word brought everything into sharp focus. This is what he had dreamed of. He reached up and caressed her face. Dawn kissed him, bringing her hands to his cheeks. "Do you understand I will always be Phillip's?" She spoke gently.

"Yes, you were never mine. But I wish to claim you in my own way. A moment shared between us, a secret that won't ever be revealed but that will warm my heart and carry me through in my dotage." Florian kissed her neck and traveled tiny bites down her chest and across the top of her dress.

"Lord forgive me, yes, claim me before I change my mind."

Florian didn't wait for the beautiful queen to change her mind. He moved between her legs and carefully lifted her dress, making certain it would not wrinkle too badly. Dawn kicked off her slippers while Florian made short work of her linen drawers and peeled them off, leaving her exposed. He lowered himself on top of Dawn, kissing her again, bringing her attention back to her desire and not that she lay semi-naked under him. Surprisingly, he felt her hands snake down his back and tug at his pants. He didn't need to be invited twice.

With expertise, he undid his trousers one-handed and pulled them down far enough to free himself. Continuing to nibble on her earlobe and whispering sweet nonsense in her ear. His cock now rested against her and he felt her slick folds part for him, a moan escaped him as the sweet moment he had dreamt about as he had stood watch came to fruition. As he tasted the sweetness of her mouth, he entered her, savoring each tiny thrust, moving stronger and fuller each time. She felt incredible as she encased him, closing around him and raising her legs to allow deeper penetration. Her moan matched his and as they found their rhythm, the room filled with quiet groans and heavy breathing.

Florian's orgasm built quickly and he moved his hips, making her buck underneath him, he knew she was close.

Their love-making halted as a male voice came through the door from the next room. "I wanted to make sure my love had everything she needed for this afternoon's ceremony." Phillip's voice could be heard.

Florian lifted his hand and put a finger on her lips as he slowly resumed his thrusting, his want growing quickly. The utter exhilaration and sheer audacity of the moment made him push into her harder, faster, raising on his knees slightly. She watched him, her bottom lip caught between her teeth, her eyes half-closed as she moved beneath him, her hips rising to match him.

They both shuddered as they silently fell over the cliff and into the abyss and clung to each other, neither able to make a sound, both of their climaxes burning his core to hers and knowing that this moment would tie them together forever. Phillip's voice was forgotten for the moment. Florian kissed her softly.

"My Lord, I can assure you that you have been generous in your desire to have Queen Dawn's every desire met, but I must follow Her Majesty's instructions and not intrude upon her at this time. She wanted to rest before the busy day ahead and we both must respect it." Florian heard Lady Hammond lie.

"Very well, please tell my lady that I called upon her."

The charming prince felt no guilt for what he had done, and he was aware that he was a step closer to his end goal. He glanced at the gold crown on the bedside table before he buried his face into the wealth of blonde hair that he had found so irresistible and whispered, "Thank you."

The officially betrothed couple led their guests from the large cathedral. It was another humid day in the Kingdom of Dreams and the sun beat down on the large gathering of nobles and other high-ranking guests as they followed the beaming couple toward the palace and the large feast that awaited them. His mother, as usual, had thought of everything and several large tables lined the pathway laden with parasols that the guests could take and use to cover themselves from the sun. Florian smiled as he overheard several guests comment on the thoughtfulness of the queen.

Florian took a parasol from Tumas, and as he opened it, he heard a polite cough behind him. He turned his head enough to see if he wanted to converse with the person trying to gain his attention. It was Wynter and his heart beat a fraction faster at the thought of spending time with her. He had been distracted through the entire ceremony, his thoughts caught between how close he was to the end of his dare and how little time he had left to complete it, but mostly filled with him trying not to stare at the wonder that was Queen Wynter. She had sat there, in the first pew, as afforded the ruling nobles of other countries, her dark hair curling softly under her chin, the colored sunlight coming through the stained-glass windows casting prisms of pretty colors upon her subdued red dress. Florian had attempted to catch her eye twice during the long ceremony, but she had been focused on the happy couple kneeling before the priest. Dawn had completely ignored him throughout the service, which he had expected. He wondered if she regretted her decision. Ashe was the opposite, smiling at him and her eyes clearly inviting him to find time alone with her at his convenience.

Wynter smirked when Florian returned her cough with a small cough of his own. At seeing the response, Florian turned a little more and smiled openly at her, not caring who saw how pleased he was to see her. "Your Majesty, would you like to share this parasol with me?"

"Why, thank you, Your Highness." Wynter stepped forward and linked her arm through his.

As Wynter's hand rested on Florian, the undercurrent he felt was clear and he could no longer ignore it. He had never felt this attraction after he had slept with anyone before. Once he had taken what he wanted, the desire usually faded, but with Wynter it continued to grow, his longing to be near her, for her to notice him almost frightened him it was so unexpected. She would leave tomorrow, and he didn't know how he felt about it.

"Is everything fine?" she inquired, quietly.

Florian looked down at her. Her cute nose was crinkled as she looked up at him, her brown eyes concerned. "Yes, of course."

"You are quiet today."

"I am?" He was surprised she had noticed.

"Yes. You would normally have engaged me in witty conversation by now."

"I am enjoying your company." He wanted to bend down and kiss her upturned lips, but the scandal it would cause would be terrible for her. She was gossiped about for taking back her throne and saying no to her predestined prince without adding kissing him in public to her list of misdemeanors. *And what happens if she doesn't want to kiss you again?* he asked himself; though, he had no answer.

"It seems every time I turn around you two are together," a voice interrupted their conversation.

Florian noted that for a brief instant something he couldn't quite categorize crossed Wynter's face before they both turned to answer Stic. "Baron Stictson, so good to see you again. I had no idea my movements were being monitored so closely," Wynter answered, her voice light, though her underlying annoyance clear.

Stic didn't look concerned by the rebuttal, he grinned at them as he matched their stride. Florian would need to get away from both of them soon if he wanted to take the opportunity the large feast would now present him to begin his heist of the ladies' three treasured items. His time was running out. Wynter and Dawn would be leaving tomorrow, and this was the last big event that would afford him the chance to disappear for a while and have no one notice him missing as there were so many people within the palace walls. He was to meet Stic at the Wild Ram Tavern at midnight.

While Wynter answered pertly, Florian went in a different direction with his friend. He answered honestly, and Stic would know it, but Florian guessed Stic would think he was working an angle with Wynter. "You find us together because I enjoy spending time with the queen; her insights and progressive thinking intrigue me."

Stic nodded and Wynter squeezed Florian's forearm gently in response to his words. He hoped she understood that it wasn't a game to him any longer, he meant what he said. They engaged in trivial conversation until they reached the steps leading up to the large open palace doors. At the top of the steps were servants ready to collect the no longer required parasols.

Florian followed Wynter into the cool entrance hall before they entered the grand ballroom off to the right. He stopped just inside the doorway and grabbed her elbow before she could move deeper into the room. One of the ever-present handsome bodyguards glowered at the touch, but said nothing. "Forgive me, Your Majesty, but I must excuse myself from your exquisite company."

Wynter smiled. "There's the sweet talker."

Florian laughed.

"I knew you were there somewhere."

"He's always lurking."

"I hope to see you later." The dark-haired beauty

winked at him. "I do have several people I need to connect with before I leave tomorrow."

Florian took her hand and brought it to his lips, formally. In just above a whisper, so no one could hear him, he spoke. "My Lady, I hope to spend a few more candle-marks with you before you must return home."

"I would welcome that." Her tone and face were serious. There was no overtone of flirting and Florian's heart thudded against his chest. What was happening to him?

Wynter's words lingered as Florian moved through the busy corridors. He greeted people that spoke to him but did not stop to talk. After extricating himself from Wynter and Stic, he had circled the room once, mingling with the guests, sipping wine, and sampling any food that was carried by. When he thought the room was full enough that his absence would not be noticed, Florian exited through a side door only to discover many nobles and merchants wandering the hallways. He didn't want people to observe where he was heading so decided to use the servants' corridors until he got closer to his rooms and his first destination. The servants would take little notice of him, and no one would think to say anything. Servants quickly moved aside as they encountered him, too busy in going about their tasks to do more than nod in his direction. Tumas and his bodyguards had been left milling around the feast as another decoy for people to believe that he was still there.

His heart raced as he thought about how close he was to

completing the threefold task and uncovering Stic's secret, and perchance the reason as to why he was acting oddly, where the ability to know the truth had come from, and why he wouldn't share how it had happened. *Don't get ahead of yourself.* He tried to calm his nerves. *Six steps completed, three to go. Focus on the next step. Ashe's diamond shoes.*

Florian made a final turn in the narrow, darkened tunnel before coming to the door he had used on his way to bed Dawn that morning, which seemed like a lifetime ago now. Dawn was now officially betrothed to his brother, Phillip, and surprisingly, Florian was happy for them both. It was always that way once he had satisfied his itch to bed someone, and there was never any ill will on his behalf, but there was typically not a want to do it again. That was why his fixation for Wynter and how much he would like to spend more time with her before she left was unsettling, and if he didn't have the pressing matter of the bet he was sure he would find it even more alarming.

As before, he stopped before the secret door and waited to hear anything. It was quiet. Florian slid open the panel and peered out. The corridor to his room was empty. Guards would be stationed at the entrance to the wing, but no one was waiting at doors, as they did when you were in your suite. He hurriedly stepped out and slid the panel closed before heading to his room. Letting himself in and making sure the door was locked behind him, Florian scooped up a velvet sack he had prepared earlier. Not wasting any time, he moved to the empty fireplace and undid a latch that looked to be part of the mantel. A book-case that stood to the side of the fireplace clicked loudly and swung a few inches outward, exposing a space behind it.

Florian lit a lantern he had put on the mantel that morning and held it high as he opened the bookcase enough for him to squeeze behind.

The darkness enveloped him, and the smell of damp and dust greeted his senses. Florian hadn't been in this space for at least eighteen years, and he remembered it being larger; of course, he was much smaller then. He took his time making his way down the short, narrow space. This little tunnel served a different purpose than the servant's corridors. This was created to join the rooms of the royal suites and it had taken him into his mid-teens to understand why it had been built. Henri and Florian had used it to hide from the governess, play pranks on their parents, and sneak into each other's rooms when they were children and in trouble. That had changed when Henri had decided he needed his privacy and had locked his side of the short tunnel many years ago.

Florian had only recalled the space that linked their rooms when he had entertained Ashe those few short days ago. As soon as he had looked at the bookshelf next to the fireplace he had recalled their forgotten childhood secret. So, after their tryst, Florian had suggested that Ashe disappear into another room so she wouldn't be seen by anyone walking by when he opened that door, when really what he was wanting was to be left alone so he could trigger the switch that had been locked by the older prince.

The lamp revealed the end of the space and Florian lowered the light to his feet to find the lever that you needed to stand on to open the bookcase from the inside. The bookcase clicked and swung open those few inches, and Florian exhaled a breath he hadn't realized he was holding. Slowly, he pushed the bookcase open, praying for no one to be in the room; though, logically, he knew they would be at the celebrations. It was always best to be prepared.

The slippers twinkled at him with the late afternoon sunlight reflecting on them. He took gloves out of his velvet bag and a long piece of velvet cloth. Florian lay the cloth on the nearest lounge and pulled the gloves on. Carefully, he lifted the clear glass case that covered the shoes and placed it on the floor. He stopped and admired the diamond slippers for a moment longer before picking up one and wrapping it in the cloth, as Florian went to pick up the other shoe he smiled to himself and chuckled softly. He decided he would only take one. It was cheeky and ironic. Technically, only one shoe was important to her as she had lost the other and that one was important to Prince Henri because he had used it to track down Ashe. Florian put the glass covering back on the single shoe, picked up the other one and put it in the sack, nestled in all its wrappings so it wouldn't break, and smiled in private triumph as he crossed the room, flicked the latch that would relock the bookcase and no one would ever suspect him.

He clutched the bag against his chest, grateful for the darkness in the small servants' corridors. The cloth of the bag against the darkness of his clothing in the dim lighting made it almost impossible for a servant to take note of it, especially as they usually diverted their eyes when he skulked by. Florian's heart raced, and unlike the thrill of the chase when courting a woman to steal her virtue, the idea of carrying stolen items from the leaders of other nations was swiftly losing its appeal. He had done daring robberies before, spurred on by Stic's dares, but while Florian crept along the tunnel he fully came to understand just what sort of international incident he could cause if caught. *Well, then don't get caught,* the arrogant side of his brain overrode the concern. *Now, relax and have fun, you are spoiling it.*

As he traversed the darkened corridors, Florian began to ponder what he was going to do with himself now everything was changing. He had not given it much thought until that moment. Phillip would leave tomorrow with Dawn, as would many of the nobles that had come for the special celebrations. And so would Wynter; though, his mind shied away from that thought. His life would return to normal, and Florian would be back to womanizing, taking idiotic and ever-growing dangerous bets to keep it interesting and being the spare heir. But that life now seemed dull and pointless. Was it time for him to grow up and take on responsibility? He smirked in the darkness. "That was a stupid thought and one that should be banished. What you need is some time away from the capital, where your drinking, whoring, and propensity for stupid challenges can find new heights," he spoke aloud.

He didn't realize anyone could hear him until he turned a corner and found a young boy pressed against the wall. "Your Highness," he squeaked as Florian moved by.

"You never saw me." Florian winked in a conspiratorial manner and smiled kindly at the page.

The boy grinned back. "Saw who?" And with those words scurried off to do whatever his assigned task was.

Florian sighed with relief. The page would do well in the palace with that sort of attitude. He noted that he would ask Tumas to track the boy down and perhaps have him assigned to the prince. A child that quick-witted was always a benefit to have in your entourage.

Around one more corner and Florian had reached the door he had been seeking. With a quick prayer to the gods of luck, Florian pushed open the panel and stepped out. His luck held and he found the wide hallway with its suits of armor, statues of animals, and large oil paintings of flowers to be empty. He stopped to make certain he could hear no footsteps approaching, and when satisfied, he moved toward Dawn's suite. He was astounded that there were no guards at her door, but then again, she was in her betrothed's home. He rapped his knuckles on the door and waited, but no one answered. Thanking every god he could name at his good fortune, he turned the handle and felt the latch click. Florian pushed the door open and entered the room, closing and locking the door behind him.

His eyes swept over the outer receiving room, noting that there was nothing of the queen in the room. All the assorted trinkets were his family's and they had been used to furnish the room to give the appearance of decadence and respect that a queen deserved. Florian knew the crown would not be in here.

After one final look around the room, he moved to the door that led through to her bedroom. He didn't bother to consider what had happened the last time he had entered this room, he had moved on from that and now had a task to complete and only candlemarks to do it in. His blood rushed in his ears at the thrill of being somewhere he wasn't invited. This was a leader of another nation's bedroom, and he was a thief no matter how charming he appeared. The thought was exhilarating, and for a moment, he wondered if he had time to find Wynter and perhaps entice her into another make-out session in one of the palace alcoves before he met up with Stic.

Florian stood in the center of the room and slowly turned in a circle, taking in the large four-poster bed, the empty bedside table where he had placed the crown this morning, the two chaste lounges, and another small table that housed a tea set and vase. The empty fireplace had the time-marking candle on it, plus several unlit lanterns, probably prepared for later tonight. He frowned as he examined every surface in the room. The golden crown with its tiered peaks at the front was not there.

A tiny flicker of panic started in his gut and Florian licked his lips as he considered what to do next. A horrible thought came to him. Had she been wearing it at the ceremony and he had not noticed because he had been too focused on Wynter? Surely not.

He reasoned through why he didn't believe she was wearing it. The ceremony had been about two people being joined as man and woman. Dawn was Phillip's equal at that moment, and the crown that announced her as queen would always symbolize her higher status than his. That was not how you wanted to start things off, and Dawn, while naive in many areas, was smart enough to know that. Phillip knew she was a queen and treated her with respect, but if they were going to make their marriage a happy one they would have to be equals in the relationship. Which meant the crown was here, somewhere.

Florian looked around the room for a second time, considering what he would do with it if he had a crown. Of course! They are leaving tomorrow, there must be a lot of packing already done. Could the crown already be packed?

In the dressing room, Florian found several open trunks, half-filled with her belongings. After taking in the room and not seeing the crown anywhere obvious, he sighed and realized that it was probably already stored somewhere in preparation for their journey home. Carefully, he started going through the trunks, making sure not to disturb anything, and it was in the third trunk that he uncovered a wooden box. He gave the trunk one last look over to memorize exactly how everything was placed so he could put it back without raising suspicion and having someone check the box.

Florian placed the clothes next to him on the floor and without taking the box out lifted the lid. He breathed a sigh of relief as the gold crown glinted in the light of the lantern he had brought in with him. Like before, with the glass slipper, Florian took out another velvet cloth and proceeded to wrap the crown before placing it at the bottom of the bag. He was careful to arrange the items in the bag so nothing broke. Quickly, he closed the box and took extra care to put everything back the way he remembered it.

As Florian stood, he laughed softly to himself. One to go.

Flicking the lock open, Florian opened the door, marveling at how his luck had held as he made his way out of the suite, pulling the door closed behind him. Florian looked to his left and was relieved to see that no one was there, then looked to his right and his heart lept into his throat as he saw two of the bodyguards in the colors of Dawn's flag marching toward him. His luck had just changed.

Florian smiled benignly and pretended that he had not been caught exiting their ruler's door. Perhaps they only saw him standing in the corridor? He walked toward them, acting as if it were completely normal for him to be about in this section of the palace. "Ah, good," he said jovially as they moved to block his path, "Can you perchance point me in the direction of the lovely Queen Wynter's door? I have a gift for her before she leaves." He held up the bag and hiccuped, hoping that his reputation for once had preceded him.

The guard on the right frowned but hesitated. "Your Highness, why were you at our Queen's door?"

Shit. They did see me.

"Oh my goodness, did I give you the wrong directions?" an innocent voice asked from behind the two burly bodyguards.

Both guards spun and revealed the diminutive Queen Wynter flanked by three of her own exceptionally hand-some bodyguards. She fluttered her dark eyelashes at the group of men before her and put on a vapid smile. "Oops. Did I say the hallway with the flowers? I meant the one with all the shields."

"No harm," Florian shrugged. "I opened the door to check you weren't in there and these gentlemen found me closing it."

Both of Dawn's guards looked uncomfortable. "We apologize for any confusion, Your Highness, but I am certain you understand that the safety of our queen is paramount."

"Of course, my soon-to-be sister-in-law is a rare gem and must be treasured. Think no more of it." He waved his hand magnanimously.

The men stepped around the prince and marched to Dawn's door and took up position on either side. Florian kept his smile fixed on his face, not showing the relief he felt at having avoided any further investigation. He bowed to the Queen of the Fourth Kingdom and spoke quietly. "Your Majesty."

"What are you up to, Florian?" Wynter looked curious.

"I was being honest," he lied. "I got the doors mixed up."

"Just not my door?" It was a pointed question.

He had no desire to hurt her feelings, but he needed to get away from her and he needed to stop the questions. "Well, I do have a reputation to keep up," he said lightly.

"Ah, yes. I quite understand. Why have one when there are many to experience?"

He was shocked by her words and his eyes flicked to the handsome blond bodyguard on her right, and the equally good-looking dark-skinned one her left. Suddenly things became clearer and for reasons he couldn't fathom, he felt slightly ill. "Your seven bodyguards are the ones you were trapped with in the forest, weren't they?"

"Yes."

"And you were all alone with nothing to do for a long time." It was not a question.

"We found things to do." She smiled sweetly. The guard on her left flashed him a smug smile. "Florian, what would you have done hidden in a forest with seven comely women?"

The prince laughed. He relaxed slightly and the ill-feeling eased. "You have me there." *Focus, fool, time is running out,* he reminded himself. It dawned on him that there could be a problem he hadn't foreseen if Wynter was heading back to her room early. "Have the celebrations become so tedious without me that you left?"

Her snort of laughter made him grin. "No, I still have nobles to charm and deals to put in place before I leave tomorrow." She winked conspiratorially at him and lifted the front of her skirts to reveal black, soft leather boots, rather than her heeled satin slippers. "My feet were hurting, so I just came to change my shoes."

"Clever."

"Well, I am off to flirt and flatter my fellow rulers into giving me what I want."

"I would wish you luck, but I know from experience that you always get what you want in the end."

"Sweet-talker. Have fun with your lady friend." Wynter smiled and moved by him, and he continued to stay in the center of the hallway, not wanting to give her a clue of where he was heading. Abruptly, she halted, and turned back to the waiting prince. She arched an inviting eyebrow at him. "Don't exhaust yourself, I have plans for you."

Florian bowed deeply, his grin wide at the suggestion. By the time he straightened, Wynter had disappeared around the corner and the hall was now empty aside from himself and Dawn's two guards.

lorian whistled loudly as he walked down the corridor as if he weren't in a hurry and had no plans for the evening. Another few minutes strolling along, and he came around the corner to where Wynter's suite was, only to discover her door guarded by two burly men. Instead of trying to backtrack he kept walking, nodded to the guards, and kept going to the other end of the short corridor, her set of rooms was the only one along this section.

The prince's mind came up with and discarded ideas rapidly as he decided how to deal with the guards. He had brainstormed this exact scenario and carried a few things on himself in case it had occurred. He looked around the quiet hallway and his eyes settled on one of the antique side tables that his mother had placed throughout the palace to hold huge vases of flowers. That could work.

The white and blue decorated vase was full of bright yellow sunflowers and Florian grunted softly as he lifted it carefully from the thin wooden table and carried it to the opposite side of the corridor and placed it next to its twin. He edged the matching vases to each end of the thin table. Florian returned to the now empty table and took out a flask of potent liquor which he poured over one leg of the table and onto the rug it sat on. "Sorry, Mother," he whispered as he took a lantern off the wall, opened it, and laid it on its side.

Florian hurried to the end of the corridor and then slowed his pace to look nonchalant as he stepped around the corner and came into view of Wynter's guards again. "Gentlemen," he nodded at them. Neither responded, but one did nod slightly. The prince kept up the charade of indifference until he reached the next corner and turned it.

Grateful to find that hallway empty, Florian spun and knelt like he was looking for something if someone approached from behind, and peered around the corner, waiting for the lantern to do its work. He didn't have to wait long when he noticed smoke curling around the far corner and crawling along the floor. Burning the palace wasn't a wonderful idea, but it was the best he had to cause a distraction when he couldn't bring in others to help him. By this point, he had seduced two women that could have profound consequences on his nation and had stolen from a queen, setting fire to a rug and table seemed trifle in comparison.

The alert guards didn't take long to notice the smoke. Florian frowned as he expected them to leave their post and investigate, but instead they knocked on the door and waited, both looking concerned, but neither abandoning their post.

Florian held his breath, willing them to go. "Come on,' he urged with a whisper. "Move."

Unexpectedly, the door to the suite opened and one of the guards turned to face the door. Florian could see his lips moving and watched as the person who opened the door stepped out to see what was going on. That guard looked at the smoke and then stepped back through the door. Florian wondered what was happening. A few moments later, the guard stepped out with another guard and they hurried down the corridor.

Florian swore colorfully under his breath as he watched the original door guards resume their position. He did a quick count and realized he should have expected that.

Wynter had three with her, there were two on the door, which meant there had been the final two bodyguards somewhere. *Sloppy thinking, you idiot.* He chewed on his lip and avoided thinking about what he needed to do for several moments but knew his opportunity would be gone if he didn't act now. Sighing with annoyance that he was about to use his secret weapon, which he had captured six months prior, he drew a tiny cage out of the sack and glared at the occupant inside. She was smart enough to remain quiet.

"I don't have time for your antics, so listen up," he whispered. "You will do precisely what I say and then I deem you free, my wish will be fulfilled, and the spell lifted. You do anything but what I tell you and you will be drawn back into this cage, and I will keep you until you learn your lesson better." He glared at the fairy who looked sullenly back at him. He waited. She nodded her understanding but crossed her arms to show her defiance. He wasn't interested in her displays of rebellion, so ignored it. "There are two vases near where the small fire is around the corner." He held the gold cage out so she could see where he meant. "I need you to push those vases over as soon as you get there, I don't want those guards thinking they can use the water in them to douse the flames." Florian held the cage up to his face. "When it is done and there are four guards in the hall you are free to leave. But," he paused. "Do not try to slip me a love potion or anything else again. You are not to be in any country I am in. Am I clear?"

Tink nodded, her green eyes flashed with anger and her face flamed red, but she fluttered her wings and waited.

"Go now." Florian opened the small door and waited.

Without looking back, the fairy's gold and green wings fluttered and she speed out of the cage, immediately rising to the ceiling and crossing over to fly above the guards' heads. Florian watched and admired her ability to understand quickly that was the best strategic way to get by. He watched the tiny glowing speck whiz around the corner and then waited, ready to spring into action and run for the door.

A huge crash filled the corridor, and the guards drew their weapons but stood their ground. The tension built and Florian prayed for them to move. He didn't know what else he could do at this point to get into Wynter's room. It has to work. The smoke had grown from wisps to a thicker consistency and was now creeping along the ceiling too.

The anticipated second crash finally came, and this time was accompanied by a shout from one of the unseen guards. Both the door guards held their swords higher, looked toward the end where Florian hid, and then took off for the other corner to check on their fellow bodyguards. This was it. Florian didn't wait, he stood quickly and as soon as the guards disappeared around the corner, he bolted for the now unguarded door. Without stopping he grasped the handle, twisted it, the door opened, and he was in. "Thank you, Tink," he whispered as he closed the door behind him. The pretty fairy had been sent by a suitor months prior to slip him a love potion in an attempt to get him to marry, but instead, had been caught because of a warning by Stic, who had seen the countess's intent while at a party one night. After consulting a crusty old magician who had sold them the gilded cage, they had set the trap, so instead of ensnaring Florian, Tink had been captured.

Florian looked around the brightly lit room. It was filled with lanterns and candles and surprisingly, three bedrolls spread out on the floor. This must be where her guards rested when they weren't on duty. He knew this was a two-bedroom suite, so assumed that one of the bedrooms was being used by several more of the guards. He decided to not do a headcount about who was sleeping where, as he acknowledged he probably wouldn't like the answer.

He walked to the right-hand door off the main receiving room, as it held the largest bedroom, and opened it. Hoping that the apple-shaped ruby Wynter had spoken of would be easier to find than Dawn's crown.

The bedroom held a large, ornate bed with tall posts on each corner. The room was tidy, but not in the same way Dawn's had been, and it was only now that Florian realized that Wynter had brought no female staff with her, no personal maids or ladies-in-waiting. *She lived in a forest for over a year with seven men, I am certain she is capable of taking care of her own needs*, he reminded himself.

Pushing the thought from his mind, Florian moved to the window and quickly unlatched it, pushing one pane wide. He wanted to make it look like that was how he was thinking he would escape.

As he moved back into the room, he looked at the large dressing table that held many pretty, jeweled items. And there, nestled amongst a gilded brush, comb, and hand mirror, and many other pretty baubles, sat the deep, red ruby, that brought to Florian's mind Wynter's full soft lips.

This was it. The final thing on the list. He guessed he had a candlemark to get out of the palace and to the tavern to meet Stic.

He had done it. Against the odds, he had done it. Florian picked up the ruby, silently celebrating his victory.

It was only when he heard her voice did he realize that she had arrived sooner than he thought she would.

"So, I save your ass and this is how you repay me?"

As he turned, Florian slipped the jewel into his waistcoat pocket and placed a pleasant smile on his face. Now to lay the bait to get her to reveal her true intentions. "Turns out my other dalliance fell through, so I decided to wait for you here."

The queen looked a little less sure of herself. "You are aware the palace is on fire, right?"

Florian spread his hands wide. "How else could I get in here to wait for you?"

TO THE WINNER...
FLORIAN

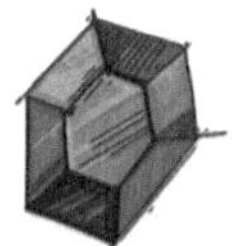

The timepiece on the bar showed it to be midnight as Florian settled into his seat. Stic beamed at him. "Didn't think you were going to make it for a moment there."

"Neither did I," Florian admitted. He needed Stic to feel overconfident.

The tavern door opened and Tumas entered carrying the black velvet sack. Two extremely handsome guards in the royal colors followed him in. Florian watched Stic give the guards the briefest look before his eyes rested on Tumas and the bag he carried toward them. Florian drew Stic's attention back to him as a third figure snuck in behind the guards and took a seat nearby, keeping their hood up. The guards positioned themselves in front of the hooded person.

A serving girl hustled over to the two seated nobles. "Bring me your best whiskey bottle, two glasses, and ask Eli to clear the room please." The girl curtsied to Florian and moved to tell the tavern owner what the prince had requested.

Florian waited, there would be no protests about forcing Eli to close his tavern; after all, Florian was a prince and his desires were never thwarted. But Eli also knew that he would be well compensated for any inconvenience by Tumas at a later date, when no one would see. The young woman returned with two glasses and the bottle before taking her shawl from a peg by the door and leaving for the night. Eli rang a bell that hung at the end of the bar, indicating it was time to go home.

Stic settled back in his chair and nodded goodbye as the usual patrons grumbled, but left once they understood the situation. No one complained, no one dared. Florian, though friendly and generous, was also a prince and it was never a good idea to be on the wrong side of one.

Eli nodded his head in their direction before he took the steps two at a time up to the second floor where he lived. If they needed anything they could come knock on the first door or help themselves.

Florian opened the whiskey and poured a finger for each of them. He held his glass aloft. "To the winner."

Stic held up his glass and clinked it against Florian's. "To the winner."

The whiskey burned as it went down and Florian savored the moment. He would finally know Stic's secret. How did his friend gain the ability to always know the truth, and could Florian do the same thing? "Shall we begin?"

"Very well." Stic put his glass down and turned his green eyes on Florian.

Florian placed his glass on the table and sat forward, resting his elbows on his knees. His hazel eyes confident as he knew he had completed every requirement. "Ask your questions."

"Did you seduce and bed Princess Ashe?" Stic began, his voice eager.

"Yes."

"Did you uncover her most treasured physical possession?" Stic's voice remained confident.

"Yes."

"Did you take it?"

This time Florian smiled in triumph, reached down, and picked up the heavy black sack. With great care, he drew out the single wrapped slipper and placed it before Stic.

Stic wasted no time in unwrapping the shoe and held it up with a quizzical look on his thin face. "Where is the other one?"

Florian smiled at his private joke. "She values that one, my brother values the other, together they make a pair."

A laugh filled the room as Tumas doubled over in amusement. "Oh, you are a devilishly clever man sometimes."

Florian felt the weight of Stic staring at him for several more moments before he nodded and put the shoe down. "I only sense the truth. We shall press on." Stic took another sip of the fiery amber liquid. "Did you seduce and bed Queen Dawn?"

"Yes."

"And?"

Without the question being asked, Florian took the weighty golden crown from the bag and unwrapped it himself before putting it before Stic. "Her most treasured possession. It represents her country's past and future."

The disappointment was clear on Stic's pale skin, and Florian stopped himself from gloating. His friend should have known better than to doubt his ability. But something has changed since Stic had gained his powers

"Did you seduce and bed Queen Wynter?" Stic sounded almost desperate.

"Yes; though, I wondered at times if it was not the other way around. That woman is surprising in her frankness." He told the whole truth, there was no point in half-lies, Stic would know if he tried to cover anything.

"You admire her?" His friend sounded interested.

"Very much so. More than anyone I have met before."

"Did you uncover her favored item?"

"Yes."

"Let's see it then."

Florian took the ruby out of his pocket and placed it on the table.

Stic stood quickly, knocking his chair backward as he did so. He whooped in celebration.

The prince ignored his friend and dug back into the bag, keeping his hands in there as he unwrapped the final item and drew it slowly from the cloth sack. Florian placed the gold hand mirror he had seen amongst her pretty baubles earlier that evening on the table and waited.

Silence fell as Stic stopped his cavorting and moved toward the mirror. He went to grab it, but Florian had anticipated it and swept it off the table before the baron could take it. "Now, now, don't be hasty, my friend."

Stic looked at Florian and then over at the guards who stood by the door. "You cheated," Stic accused.

"How?"

"You said the ruby apple was her favored thing, you can't change your mind and present another item when I showed my hand and celebrated because you got it wrong."

Florian smiled his disarming smile and spoke calmly. "Actually, I did no such thing. You asked if I found out what her prized possession was, all I said was yes. I took out the ruby but never said that was it. You jumped to that conclusion all on your own." He looked in the hand mirror and saw how his hazel eyes glinted in the firelight; he was enjoying himself immensely. "It just so happens that her most valued object is you," Florian spoke the words softly.

Stic paled further than his usual pallid features and sat heavily on his chair. "Me?" he asked; though, he didn't seem surprised.

"Yes, you," Wynter spoke as she moved out from behind the two guards and pulled her hood back. "I have missed you and your truth. I have been searching for you, my friend."

Florian watched his friend and it seemed as if there was an internal struggle taking place. Stic began to speak, but it was in a deeper tone than his usual voice. "The evil one cast me out of my safe space to float in this world because I only see the truth, and no matter how many times she asked, it never changed. When she realized you lived still, she went mad and blamed me, using her magic to release the binds that kept me in the mirror." Stic shuddered. "I was lost and scared. I had no anchor and then I found this." The baron pulled out a heavy chain from under his shirt that held a white crystal in a claw setting. "It called to me as a haven and I entered it, but it held different powers than the mirror and I found I had control of this body."

"But what was the point of all the games, challenges, and bets?" asked Florian.

"I am simply a mirror for the truth. I see to the heart of things." Stic stared at him. "I was a mirror to you. The more you wanted to push yourself, the more I pushed you. The more you needed to prove your abilities, the more you wanted me to issue bigger challenges, and I complied. You want to be desirable to everyone, so you became desirable to Stic."

Florian shook his head trying to understand what Stic—no, the being that lived in the crystal, was saying. He had brought this on himself because of his ever-increasing ego. He could have destroyed everything because of his insecurities at being a third-born prince. Those were thoughts he kept to himself. Finally, Florian understood. The mirror only responded with the truth of what it saw. *You also had the ability to not accept the challenge in the first place,* his inner voice whispered. *You set your home on fire, people could have been hurt, all to prove what?* The thought hung there, but there was no answer.

Wynter cleared her throat. "Would you return to the mirror and serve me, old friend?" she asked.

"Willingly, if there was a way." Stic looked forlorn and lost.

"The ruby is the way. One apple almost claimed my life, but this one can return it." Wynter turned to Florian and held out her hand. He handed over the mirror without a word of protest. He watched her place the mirror face-up on the table, then place the ruby apple on the mirrored surface before taking the crystal necklace from the baron, which she also placed on the reflective surface.

The queen of the Fourth Kingdom looked to Stic. "You might want to brace yourself for this. I am not quite sure what will happen." She held her petite hands over the assembled treasures and closed her brown eyes and began to chant. "Mirror, mirror, gold and small, it is the fairest one of all. I have the apple whose curse befall, it is the spirit that I recall."

Florian felt the room constrict as if the air had been sucked out of it. The fireplace spluttered and several candles went out. It was only for a moment, but it was enough to make him believe in all the legends and curses he had always scoffed at. When suddenly, he could breathe again. He watched as his friend slumped forward in his chair, banging his head on the wooden table before slipping sideways and tumbling from his seat. Tumas rushed to his aide as Florian decided to save Wynter as she too lost consciousness and slid off her chair. He managed to get to her before she hit her head on anything and he lowered her to the flagstone floor, where he cradled her in his arms.

"What happened?" Stic asked as he slowly sat up with the aid of Tumas.

"How much do you remember?" Florian asked.

Confusion showed clearly on his face. "I don't know." His voice sounded strained. "What day is it? How much did I drink?" The baron looked at the queen in his friend's arm. "Pretty lass you have there. Who is she?"

Trying to not sound alarmed at the clear evidence that Stic had no recollection of being possessed by the mirror,

Florian decided that the best course of action would be to have him rest for now and explain once he had recovered from the head knock, or not explain at all. He looked down at the sleeping woman and admired her beauty. She truly was the fairest of all. "Get Eli to make up several rooms, we shall be staying here tonight," he ordered one of the men. The guard headed upstairs. Florian looked to the other one. "Let the four bodyguards that stand outside the door know that we are staying here tonight. They can decide if they need to inform the other three or let them stay up at the palace."

Florian looked down at Wynter and gently shook her. "Wynter?" he said softly, almost as if he was calling her. "Wynter, my love, you need to wake up." The words were so quiet he was confident that no one would hear them.

"What's happening?" A strong male voice spoke from the mirror. "Someone hold me up so I can see."

Tumas propped Stic up on his seat while they waited for the rooms to be prepared, then took up the mirror, turning it to face the prince.

"I don't know what to do," Florian spoke to the mirror.

It shimmered as it spoke. "Yes, you do."

"You have got to be kidding? I am not suitable," Florian protested.

"The choice is always yours; she has demonstrated this before." The mirror spoke firmly. "Choose now."

Florian ran his finger over the blood-red lips of the queen, across her pale white cheek and traced around her ear, and moved his hand into her straight black hair. She was truly intoxicating. Without further hesitation, he bent down and pressed his lips to hers, willing her to wake. A soft groan escaped her lips as she responded, and he moved to pull away, but she wound her hand around his neck and held him firmly against her lips. After a few passionate moments where he lost his senses, they pulled apart and her eyes flickered open. "You kissed me awake." She smiled up at him.

"Yes, I hope you are not disappointed."

"I want to know something," Wynter said as she snuggled deeper into the crook of his arm.

"Mmmm?"

"Why do it?"

Instantly Florian was wary. "That is a loaded question. Why do what, exactly?"

"Why take on challenges that could damage your relationship with your family, or even worse destabilize the nation if you slept with or pranked the wrong person?"

"Boredom."

"I don't buy it." Wynter pushed herself up on her elbow and rested her head in her hand.

"To beat Stic?"

"Nope. You uncovered his secret, but that, in the end, was just another challenge to you. Nothing more, really. Were you not bedding women you shouldn't before the mirror and its ever daring challenges came along?"

Florian was becoming uncomfortable. He didn't like self-reflection. "Will you accept, for the sheer fun of it? Sex is always great, after all." He reached up and caressed her face, hoping to divert her attention from the topic she had raised.

Wynter chuckled. "You don't need to tell me how great sex is, remember?"

"Ah, yes. The woman stuck in a tiny cabin with seven men for a year."

She dragged her fingernails across his chest, digging in a little more than most women would. His cock responded. "You are clever, charming, handsome and," she murmured as she lowered her head to take his nipple into her mouth.

"And superfluous," he supplied.

Wynter swirled her tongue before lifting her head to look into his eyes, they held understanding and something more. "Tell me." She looked earnest as if she wanted to hear what he said.

Florian watched her. This was a queen, a woman who had been hunted and cursed and hidden away. She had made her own destiny by rejecting the one laid before her by the fates when she had shunned the advances of the charming prince who had kissed her awake as the prophecy had planned, and now Florian had kissed her awake and he didn't know what that meant. "It pales in comparison to what you have faced. Now when I think about it, it was purely bratty behavior that set me on this path." As the words were spoken he saw how true they were.

The stunning Queen of the Fourth Kingdom kissed him softly, her lips barely touching his. "Let me decide for myself."

"You are going to have to stop doing that if you want me to talk about anything." He cupped her jaw and ran his thumb along the swollen lips he appeared to be obsessed with. "I am loved. I know I am loved. My mother has always made it clear that I was wanted."

Wynter caught his thumb between her teeth and sucked on it sensuously for a moment before allowing him to withdraw it. "Am I boring you?" he asked, his tone light.

"No, I just find you irresistible." She moved back to resting on her elbow, her head in her hand. "I'll behave, go on."

"You sure? Because I am happy to put this aside for another time and ravage you instead."

She smirked at him. "Nice try; though, a good ravaging sounds mighty fun, I want to know more about you first." Her heart-shaped face grew serious. "Talk."

"Henri was born to be king. He will make a brilliant king and Ashe will be the perfect queen for him. He has been groomed and educated in everything he will need to know. Phillip was raised to lead armies and protect us from many enemies. He spent his youth becoming the most accomplished warrior amongst our soldiers. And then there was me. The third-born son to a king who had no real use for him. I was schooled as anyone high born should be, and given the same lessons as my brothers in many areas. But I learned quickly that though I was wanted by my parents, I was not needed like my brothers were. I am qualified to rule a kingdom or to ride into battle and marshall armies, but I have neither." His voice was soft as he admitted his truth. "I will always be second best to my brothers."

"I have spent time with both your brothers, and you are far more capable at putting people at ease than them. They command respect, but you engage in a different way and earn respect just as easily."

"My mother said I could always charm my way into or out of anything. So one day when I was sixteen, a Duke came to court with his daughter, looking for a marriage proposal from someone suitable. She was eighteen and pretty and I had recently discovered sex, thanks to a young chambermaid. I decided that while she tried to capture some young or not so young lord's eye, I would see if I could bed her with the understanding that I would not be marrying her. Was I really as charming as my mother proclaimed?" Florian stopped and looked at Wynter.

"So this is how you proved yourself? By bedding women and setting more and more outrageously difficult tasks?"

Florian shrugged. "I did warn you. I am not a hero, a savior, or anything special."

"Now that Phillip is marrying Dawn you are the spare heir until Ashe has a child," Wynter pointed out.

And with those few words, the coin dropped. The few odd looks that he couldn't fathom what Ashe was thinking now made sense. She had not slept with him because she found him desirable enough to chance ruining her marriage, nor did she continue to pursue him for those reasons. She had slept with him on the off chance that he could get her pregnant as Henri had not been able to do it so far. She would give her husband a child with royal blood and an heir. Florian let out a long, slow breath as he worked through his feelings. It turned out that Ashe was far more willing to do what she must for her husband and the crown than anyone would ever guess. Good for her, and if she does fall pregnant he had no intention of revealing what part he played.

Wynter interrupted his musings. "You do know that one

day your cavalier choices and devil may care attitude will come back to bite you on the ass?" Wynter's look was grave.

Florian stretched his arms over his head, feeling his shoulders pop as he looked at the beautiful queen with who he had become smitten. "As long as it's your teeth doing the biting, I'm game."

"You really are incorrigible. I think I may become bored without you." She raised an eyebrow at him. "Have you ever considered visiting the Fourth Kingdom?"

His wicked grin was all the answer she got as the charming thief reached for her.

If you enjoyed the book please consider leaving a review on your favourite place to purchase and/or Goodreads and/or Bookbub.

This helps the author immensely.
Don't forget if you want to receive information,
news and exclusive offers please sign up for the

Taya Rune Newsletter:

https://www.tayarune.com/subscribe

ACKNOWLEDGMENTS

I would like to take a few moments to say thank you to the people who have supported me along this journey.

To my husband, thank you for being my partner in crime.
I love the way you still make me laugh.

To my children, thank you for teaching me to let go of the small stuff.
I am proud of you.

To my family, thank you for the love and support you have shown me throughout the years.

To my friends, the ones that have my back and are forever in my corner
I cherish you.

To my editor, Rochelle J. Simas –
IDK art.

Thank you for the kind words that always accompany the return of my fabulously edited manuscripts.

To my PA – Book Queen.
Thanx for doing so much of the behind the scenes heavy lifting for me.
I am forever grateful for you.

To my ARC, Street and Beta Teams.
You rock!

To my cover designer - SWEET 15 Designs.
My covers look amazing thanks to you.

To my formatter - BBB Publishings.
Thank you for always squeezing me in and making my books look professional.

And to my readers, thank you for your continued support, it means the world to me. Xox

ABOUT TAYA RUNE

Taya Rune is a writer of romance, a sucker for happy endings and has a knack for asking people uncomfortable questions.

She is a member of the Romance Writer's of Australia and has had her work published in different anthologies and publications.

Taya resides in Melbourne and loves the unpredictable weather, the varied cultures, food, and great stage shows, and that there is always something new to experience.

Pinterest:

https://www.pinterest.com.au/TayaRune